AF411098

Life of an Angel

Life of an Angel

Vidara Liyanage

Copyright © 2021 Vidara Liyanage

All rights reserved.

ISBN : 978-624-97805-0-7

DEDICATION

This book is dedicated to my class teacher Mrs. Oska Prasadhi Weerasena and to all the people out there who will read and enjoy this story with heaps of love and best wishes.

Table of Contents

Join together with Angel Ivy on this Epic adventure….

Her story;

1. Beginning

I Was never the type to enjoy the long, chilly and almost dreadful duty walks along the leafless shrubbery in raw twilight with hideous creatures running to and fro in my path, blocking my way and sometimes getting on my most intense nerves. Still, I had no other alternatives in my world. Angels who disregard responsibilities and obligations are bound to grave retributions and there's no mean of escape or decamp. That's the mandate common to each and everyone including even the higher-ups and top ranking nobles. Drenched by the unsympathetic downpour along with nipped fingers and toes, I continued. It wasn't that I felt cold or anything just merely loathsome. With a sincere mind I engrossed myself on the most cardinal duty of all which is carrying the half-dead to our world. Performance of the relevant exploit and later sipping out their dearest souls and embodiments was also to be done as a time honored custom. All in all, it seemed like a typical day of work. There was nothing compulsive or out of the box just the standard stuff like somber clouds all over which normally spread far and wide and on the other hand, penetrating showers above my skull but not to mention at least the king-size pile of brain racking work. (Reader, up to now you wouldn't have had the faintest clue of what or who I am. So, remember this as you proceed on with my story,....I am an Angel, a guardian in-charge of half- dead humans) As this is my work I Angel Ivy the great and glorious, proceeded towards the pale, motionless figures with blank expressions moving from post to pillar. They looked gaunt and slightly out of focus, not as if they were defunct or anything but they looked, well....perfectly ALIVE! (According to my own line of argument that is....)The dead were coming....towards me, earnestly waiting to be taken away from their ghastly lives of misery. Now, as I had gone ahead and had a closer of field vision and a much better outlook, I could see that they looked faded and much more like air that moved instead of having the appearance of anyone with life. First and foremost, came forward an old hag. Although, well dressed but yet looking distressingly ancient at the same time. Well....anyway she seemed at least a fourscore even though the haunted impression on her wrinkled face gave her a macabre look of a millennium. She was comparing acceptable from what I generally got. At least she wasn't tempestuous, wild or boisterous and didn't look at the least bothered from departing that I, Angel Ivy threw a sign of great relief and solace. (Reader, I know some of my narrations are slightly exaggerating but do try to cope with it until the very end….) I held on firmly to the bloodless almost skeletal hand. It was cold, bony and very likely. And as I did, she threw me a feeble yet savage glance which seemed quite unnoticed at first, I looked back at her and returned a grin making my first impression as if I didn't care and before I knew it we were lingering at a leisurely pace. After a few bleak and doleful hours, I returned back and that was the end of that particular old dame. She was gone, vanished and by now completely out of sight. It's a pity. Being only a newbie it was quite difficult at first but yet fortunately my wits have sharpened through endless experience and not getting depressed about my work really helps now that the duties have become habitual. I proceeded…..still having much more of this drudgery before I could even envision of returning back to my dull and tedious abode, the heavenly realm. I galloped forward in order to witnesses my next casualty. There was just so many were there to choose from, a copious amount to be exact, both the long-in teeth and the off springs. Trying not cock-up, I cudgeled my smarts and thought hard while eventually decided to go first with a neurotic fourteen year old, a gawky red haired teen, vulnerable and wild eyed with two yellow fangs sticking out ferociously more prospective to a wild, feral animal rather than a human being even a dead one. As I examined closer…. I got a better glimpse of the ambitious face. Pale and slightly freckled he was flashing his jet black eyes which glittered venomously in the twilight. He was ragged and barefooted that

I felt merciful deep down. This young lad must have led a calamitous, gruesome life and his existence must have been immoral, I assumed. Still, I pushed my sympathetic solicitudes away as if they were crimes or felony and with an unsettled mind, I resumed….Then, I tried to grab the young whippersnapper gently by the wrist. To be precise, I'm not actually the gentle or tender-hearted type. Without a second thought, the lad seized it ferociously away from mine. What a muscular refusal it was? It was kind of brawny with comparison to his age. I was neatly shaken and was thrown into the thick bushy heather and barely managed to get on my own two feet again. And as I stood up, 'well….never mind!' I muttered to myself. 'Control yourself Ivy, It's just a kid. The lad is just a small fellow right? No harm done!' I took a few deep breaths trying to appease my anger and vexation without letting it show since neither of us was allowed to express emotions while on duty. I approached the juvenile again, 'Well…. everybody should go away once they die right? It's not like he's immortal.' I repeated again and again in order to conciliate myself. I wasn't habitually magnanimous just more of the cheeky and impertinent type which exasperated and usually got me on the abominable side of superiors. Yet, I could tranquilize the resentment much better this time as the circumstances felt unorthodox and the stripling was an outcast. Anyhow he seemed unique in his own way; I guess it is uncanny but one way or another I cherished his sentiments, strange enough. But this time with much more sangfroid and tact I tried to approach him. The first half went fairly well, he wasn't aggressive but still he didn't move either. The lad just stood still as a doomed status. I am not particularly good at dealing with kids of his age, so assuming that the awkward not loquacious silence and less of action meant he had given in and is ready to depart was a grave, perilous misapprehension and it didn't take long for me to realize that either. Just a matter of time when the kid.... reminders of that spine chilling juncture just gives me the goose bumps even today, how immature of me) It was an inhuman, barbaric and homicidal act which was absolutely unpredictable, especially from a teen. (Reader, I hope you are anticipating my state of mind this very instant. What shame it is and exceedingly remorseful on my behalf for a guardian spirit awaiting longingly to be promoted to the position of Ministering Angel to be outwitted plus out busted by a commoner, what would god-in charge think of me? Will he consider me hare-brained? Or would it probably get worse?) This is what happened; without thinking twice or at the very least once, the barbarian charged....flying towards me aiming straight to the neckline. It was just half an inch above the throat and missed it by Nano seconds. There weren't any expressions, fear or any invitational smirks on the brutal face. It was unreadable as it lacked emotions, not that I expected any. Yet, the menacing eyes were blazing with dead cruelty. Moreover, one thing was concrete, he was a lion in a fight and I, Ivy was his foe. His clawed hands grasped my neck, my throat and held it across his mouth drawing the blood out using the sharp canines. He was muscularly, as strong as an ox. Blood splattered almost everywhere among the battle field. I roared in anguish and attempted to break free, grabbing his head and pushing it down. He fell....harshly, crashing against the ground with a huge 'thud'. He was thrown flat in the face. I was lucky to get away with just a small bleeding slice even though I had lost tons of blood. My raw wound bled openly, meanwhile a sudden gush of pain jolted throughout my body while my bitten neck lost tension and my legs felt weak. I was limp and out of breath. It was near fatal. Yet I reconciled….my arm was numb for a moment or two. My ears rang while my eyes eagerly wanted to pop out of their sockets….while the blood dripped warmly down my neck. I couldn't take this anymore. Whatsoever, It soon healed, panting as I did…. 'What the heck! Darn it….Belligerent! You lunatic, you punk! You are good as dead now!' I exclaimed to myself. 'No more miss goody!' I lacked depth but not anymore. I wasn't going to let this continue anymore. No way have I ever been treated like this. Shit! I wanted to torture him now and that was obvious, if it is that last thing I do…. The once sympathetic solicitudes were gone and by now completely vanished in to thin air. It was revenge….and hatred that soaked me now.

In that frozen second between standoff and fighting, I saw his eyes flick from me to him. He looked the same, nothing had changed. But I have. His tongue was soaked in the taste of my very own blood. Still, there was no fear as I had expected. But I will make sure there will tears and loads of that too. He will get down on his feet and 'plead mercy'. I was hooked, completely absorbed by savage, revenge and unobvious thoughts. (I won't continue as some are quite offensive) My body was now filled with butterflies. I was excited; electrified....I just realized the rumbling eco. The weather had worsened, perfect for a straight up iconic brawl. I charged with a mighty cry....I wasn't going to let it go with just a mere fist fight. By now, the juvenile was lying on ground. I charged with a mighty cry....pulled him to his feet while nearly tearing off the collar. I lunged forward, quickly sprinting towards him trying to cleave his legs. I was going for a blunt force punch this time vial, disposal and vigorous. He darted back, swinging left then right. I ducked forward, attempting a direct hit right across the nose but reflex kicked in....I was making a serious attempt, which proved not to be easy for a second or two. I wondered if all this strain was worth it. He was strong. Yet, I wasn't backing off. It's either hook or crook. But....victory was uncertain as it is. His fist smashed against my shoulder, numbing my arm again for a moment. But, I successfully backed off....A few awkward moments passed by....with several unspoken words. 'You have brazen confidence.... great!' I murmured. 'If I am to die, I shall fight to the last breath', with renewed vigor he hissed in his raw, hallow voice. 'Else let me live....a bit longer....I have unfinished business'. He was clawing his hands again but by now I just wanted to finish this off quickly as I had wasted enough time already. I darted forward again. He too struggled but kept on advancing, he wasn't giving up for sure. He really wanted to live, but is his life worth living? There was no time to loose as he trotted forward. I grabbed his throat without the blink of an eye; his neck and the nearly torn collar were in my fullest control as I had the fellow enveloped in my arms. It was my spotlight to finish him off….forever. But the answer ran through my head much more clearly in a way that I had never ever expected. 'Let him live, let him live, you won't regret it.' But, No! I said to myself. Never! After what he had done to an Angel, never! I jabbed his collar but my hand shook. Again the answer came. 'Let him live. Let him live. You won't regret it.' Without a clear decision, I let him off the hook. But I wanted to grab him again. Yet I didn't dare to as he belonged to himself once again. 'I will let him go, and live his life again', I thought. 'He deserved it, I will let him win. But what would god-in-charge say?' several thoughts flooded in my head. Will I get disciplined? Never! It won't happen. I was sure of my instincts. 'Flee!' I said. 'Get out of here. Get lost! Live, live your life! Go away! And get to that quickly, I will forgive you! Take this opportunity before my mind changes. Go! Go! Leave and never return and don't leave any signs. Live your life. Your life won't finish here! Go, live your life, be free! Be happy! Your own confidence would backfire you one day but until then consider it as a gift from above', I cried. 'A friend from afar had helped you today. Now go! And leave no regrets but yet have no farewells either!' (This wasn't what I was supposed to do, but I will go with my instincts for now.)

'Am I right? Did I do the right thing?' Surely, this was going against regulations. I began to question myself several times. But my heart knew what I had just done and is going to do is right, at least right enough for me. 'Don't you dare think of repaying me? You have caused enough trouble already. GO! And do not have any lingering attachments to me or for what I had just done. Go now! What are you waiting for? Don't you understand….Are you dumb? Go!' I said. 'Never come back! Don't ever show that face in front of me again. Leave!' Though the complexities of human emotions are a mystery to us Angels, we do understand one thing and that is how to make deals and stick to our words.

'You certainly have no shame Miss Angel.' But yet I could feel the happiness, the gratitude, the thankfulness inside his voice. It was no longer cruel. For a second or two, he sounded like a normal kid. Taking a few steps back he bowed, which certainly expressed his unspoken words of gratefulness. Yet, he didn't say a word. But his body expressed it all. I was happy; as it was the right thing anyway….

'Thank You, Miss. I will repay you, someday at least. I owe you my life miss,' he said finally. 'Then I'd have to live very long, right? I mean for you to pay me back. But do not misunderstand. I am doing this so you will suffer.' I said. 'You really have a way with words miss...' said the juvenile. 'You are a witty kid...enough blabbering nonsense now. Make haste and go, finish what you have to do....before I alter my mind and it's a matter of time before I do.'

'I will get going then miss....'He gave a little gentleman–like bow again and turned to go. Little by little, he vanished and now was completely out of sight, out of my field of vision. Soon he disappeared. I was left alone in the battlefield. A winner or looser couldn't be decided. But it was still a looming victory and definitely not an imminent defeat. I was over the moon. This was the kind of good deed; I had longed to do for a very long time. Yet with much hesitation, I had finally done it. I was so happy. But my saintly thoughts got interrupted as my wounded neck sent out a gush of pain throughout my insides, the upper level of my body got completely paralyzed with pain. I still bled....I had forgotten about it for a minute or two. 'Whoa! Darn it! Damn, that badass child....How I despised him!'(Reader...by now you might have guessed I had gone overboard with a dead body. But believe me it happens. You see...even though we address them as dead bodies, they are not completely dead, to finish them off is a duty of an Angel of my state) Anyway....this incident had brought in same agitation in to my monotonous life. It is secretive. Yet I cherished it. The wound on the other hand, will definitely leave a mark as the sharp-edged canines had seeped deep down the flesh. Suddenly, a voice echoed inside my head reminding that I still had much more to do, before I could finish off for the day and surely neglecting them wasn't a choice. I had dealt with only two victims so far even though hours had passed. How did time fly by so fast? This wasn't going to do, if this goes on I'll never get done at all. I guess the worst is over but there's much more to come. 'Who knows what I'll get next, may even be an assassin like yesterday or may even be a psycho like always? I was a bit fatigued than usual but yet preceded forward to witness who was next in line, wishing it wasn't strenuous or laborious work. I galloped forward, whoever it was I hope I'd get done quickly. I proceeded……

'Hands up! I'll shoot or else stop the car…!' Snap crack Bang! Bang! Bang! What was that? The sound shook me, I looked around. But I couldn't catch a thing as there wasn't anything in close vicinity. But surely I was not to get involved. Not this time. I already had enough trouble upon my own sleeve to last for a very long time to come. Snap! Crack! Bang! Bang! The sound came again, echoing through the woods, renting the still country air. The noise reverberated in the ears and ran out from over the hills. Snap! Crack! Bang! Bang! The sound came again. From the loudness, I estimated the shooting was less than five hundred meters away. More worryingly, the rapidity of the shots suggested some automatic. I pierced my ears hoping for more noise. Yet, nothing happened, everything quieted. Then, the silence returned far more thickly than it was before the shots as if everything around me was collectively holding it's breath and begging me not to get involved. I didn't want to know what it was either as it was sure to be serious trouble. Yet, I was curious. Various thoughts swam deep inside my mind, 'what was that sound, was there a fight? Who is fighting? What could it be? Could this be fatal? Did someone get shot? Who is the villain? Who got shot?' My instant reaction would have been to find out the cause. Yet, I backed off thinking more sagaciously. I seriously did not want more trouble. So I pushed the thoughts back and continued….No more were said nor heard about the shots or whatever they were. I resumed…'I was getting too much distracted these days,' I thought. 'And these incidents were surely not helping either', I said to myself. 'No more hindrances. Not even the slightest interference would stop me now. Even if the heavens fall down from the sky, I won't rest until I finish my duty'. With this strong resolution, I resumed…. Thankfully, the next half of duty wasn't as stressful or difficult as the first and it finished much quicker than expected. Firstly, I had to deal with a decorated Roman soldier wearing a shiny loose fitting helmet and a sword, gleaming with pride. However his purple face was filled with cruelly cut wounds. Also, was the white jagged end of a broken bone cutting through the skin and blood running freely in thick scarlet rivers amongst the hair of his leg. He was a bloody mess yet he stood straight in pride and in extreme patriotism for his motherland. He was half dead, half alive, but I wasn't going to judge that. I had no intention in dragging a conversation, but wanted to finish him off without a word to spare. He was a broken ruin but you should never judge a book by its cover. On his last moment he got on his knees and used his final drop of breath to shout, 'For the peace and prosperity of the land we live in. Salute!' I let him utter his death wish but after a few minutes, without any hesitation I held tightly the muscular hand and then again after few more minutes, he was just a memory once and for all. No Regrets, he died as a warrior. I was almost finished by now, just a few more minutes and I'll be returning home. It wasn't much of a home, I meant that it wasn't a happy place but yet it was still my abode. However I wanted to go back as quickly as I could. I never liked this work, just compelled to do it by nature. According to myself taking a life out of a human is something unbearable. It was all because I believed in the 'Dignity of Life'. Still, experience and daily practice had hardened me up.

Snap. Crack. Bang! Bang! Help! Help!

The enigmatical sound could be heard again. Surely, it was multiple shots…. This time much louder than before, but now it was accompanied by a bloody cry of pain, from a feminine voice.

Bang! Bang!

More gunshots could be heard again. The curiosity inside my body increased vividly. I really wanted to check it out, solve the mystery, and be the heroine. But the unknown voice in my head echoed again, 'Ivy, stay focused! Stay focused! Do what you should but nothing more,' came the voice in side my head. 'What am I thinking? I shouldn't get involved or I will get disciplined again for meddling in human affairs.'(The thought of living in a dark, damp cellar room with only stale bread and water instantly put me off the idea and I cared no more) Fortunately, the sound stopped and again no more could be heard while nothing more was said. I continued again....I turned to face my last casualty for the day and saw a signora, wearing an evening gown while smiling in an after -dinner mood. She was sophisticated, ostentatious and lavish. The lady was a fancy pants and really not my preferable type either. Still, I went closer and grabbed her wrist....'Stare alla largo la ragazza'(Keep off Girl) 'what!' I said. 'In English please,' I requested. 'Keep off the stitches, Girl! Its hand made and of the best silk in Italia', she said in a prestigious high-toned voice. 'The stitches, really? The timing is strange'. Yet, I wasn't indignant. 'Alright, signora….' No more roughhouses, I thought. What she wants, she'll get. It's her final wish anyway…. I placed my hand a bit lower, safely away from her clothing and held on firmly. She was perfectly still and didn't cause any trouble either. But yet, 'Addio! La mia bella terra'. (Farewell! My beloved land) she said in ringing notes and totally out of pitch .And she was gone, forever! Never to be back ever again!

'Finished, at last! What a day!' It surely was a very laborious day. But now, everything was over. I was glad…. 'And now, time to return.' I said do myself as I breathed relief. By now, I was faintish from exhaustion. I had long ceased to get rid of my duties, even though it proved futile. The cloudburst had stopped too; maybe it had stopped a few hours ago or may be even earlier. Yet, I failed to notice anything cause the tension in myself. As I turned my back to go, I witnessed….

It was nature's most magnificent illustration bathing the world with liquid gold. By now, the sky was dyed in pomegranate pink. It was like sun's fiery kiss good bye to the day and welcoming the night with open arms. I stood….gazing with awe, the sun falling behind the horizon while listening to chirruping of birds in silhouettes flying across a sky that was now magenta. The mauve of the dusky sky intensified…. I was obsessed by the sight which gorgeous and truly magnificent. 'Breathtaking!' I said. It was much more than just a masterpiece of nature; sunsets were always my escape to the reality. It brought back blurred memories of watching a summer sunset from a spot, similar to this near the line where heavens touched the earth. Not so very long ago, just a lifetime. I just stood watching and as I did....

The fiery golden orb painted the sky with red and pink. The colors were like symbols each showing what tomorrow would bring. The sun dipped down lower and lower as time passed by...the last grasp of beauty before the death of the day. It was a glorious conflagration, blazing with a wide range of colors yet producing no warmth. The rays were destined to brighten my life. As I stood...My heart sang with indescribable notes. As, I admired the wonders, my soul expanded in the worship of its creator. I was lost in the moments, completely absorbed. The sun lingered a bit more, then dipped over, kissed goodbye and was gone. It was a marvelous sight that nothing can replace. Every sunset brings promise of a new dawn. They reminded me that I want my life to be an inspiration to others, walking in rivers of kindness extending grace and seeing other people not through my eyes but through my faith. My spirits soared....far away, more far than I could ever imagine. My eyes drifted to rest as they if had been blinded by the truly magnificent sight. It was finished now....The colors of the sky were now hidden with the black despair of the night. As I was about to leave....I thanked God, that this day had come and gone. All the pain, all the despair and the ton of spoken words, Everything Gone! Vanished into thin air! It was like proof that no matter what happens, whatever you face, every day can end beautifully, with much hope. Thank you nature! It was my reward for surviving another day in this world of cruel men. (Reader....By now you might have wondered if I had forgotten the mysterious thunder of gunshots or whatever they were but the curiosity didn't leave my body. I wanted to find out what it was. The mystery remained… in my head)

2. Strange Happenings

The shadows were already dissolved into the night time velvety darkness. The once liquid gold sky had automatically transformed into a vast expanse of jet-black covered with a canopy of luminous stars materialized amongst the ocean of blackness, just giving off enough light to illuminate the dark, moonless night. When, suddenly bang! Bang! Boom! A shot thundered across and then again a few more....Bang! Bang! Each one were not simply loud, they cracked into the air and echoed, magnifying my feelings of astonishment. But this time, I was inconsistent....I was just too anxious to back off without finding out what it was or who could the devil be to cause such a ruckus. 'Focus, Ivy! Focus!' cried the voice inside my head.

Yet, I lost control again….Bullets tore through the woods, sending splinters flying angrily. I took a few steps aback, afraid of making the slightest peep. 'What was happening? What's going on?' something quite serious was happening and not far off either….I took a deep breath. I exhaled. I inhaled again. I could feel the discomfort of curiosity spreading throughout my body like a deadly virus which controls the whole wide world. Focus, Ivy Focus! With much hesitation, I realized that this was not something I could just pass by with folded hands as I believed in the dignity of life; I had to keep my oath as an Angel. I preceded….Took a few more steps, stopped and again took a few more. I stood hidden among the bushy part of the shrubbery, making sure I was not seen and in a way in which I could get a secretive glimpse of the incident.

A man in black continued advancing, he looked neither left nor right. He just advanced….He was like a terrorist invading a new land. Drifting right then left he advanced forward. His body language showed that he knew what he was doing. Bang! Another shot thundered. He was alone….But he had a gun, an automatic revolver. The shots I heard earlier, might have aroused from that particular gun. Yet, he did not seem capable of fighting; I was frozen stiff. I couldn't make out whatever was happening two meters in front of me. I was a spectator, I didn't dare to move. Yet, I was sure this wasn't leading to anything pretty. I stood watching, trying figure out on which ground he was on. The man in black advanced again….Everything was happening lightening fast. It took some time for me to absorb it all. Then, there was a momentary disruption…This was well planned and that was concrete. Third of a second later….The scene really came to life as he dug onto his pocket, pulled out a Saturday night special and began to shoot, with the automatic revolver on his right and the Saturday night special lowered in his left. He pivoted his head, and took small steps backward towards where I stood. 'Had he seen me? Had I given the game away?' But he did not stop where I was shrouded. The mysterious figure kept moving ahead, further and further. I stood glued to the ground, daring not move. Either he hadn't noticed my appearance or just pretending not to. Yet, I had to be careful. He proceeded further and further not noticing me. And vanished…. 'Was that it?' I couldn't understand a thing. 'What just happened? Who was he? And where was he now? Whom did he shoot?' The second party was nowhere to be seen. 'Was this another unsolved mystery?' I couldn't make out head or tail. 'What just happened?' The rest was accompanied by an awkward silence. Hours passed. More hours flew by. Yet, nothing happened. Just silence, nothing more. 'Was this a dream, surely it wasn't? Was it?' I had to pinch myself in order to guarantee that I'm awake and not dreaming. Time flew yet nothing happened. The trees were still swaying in the wind and leaves still rustled against the ground. I decided to wait a bit more. Hours flew little by little. Yet, there was nothing out of the ordinary. Finally midnight came, now the darkness was almost absolute and to complete it was the dead silence which filled the melancholic night. Only a smattering of luminous stars scattered the heavens. Even the moon had been obscured among the pitch black clouds. I couldn't even see myself clearly as the whole world had lost color. It was like the calm before the storm. I decided to wait a bit longer. Maybe, the stranger in black would return. Time flew. Yet, no one came….With much shillyshally, I made the decision to leave.

There was no point in waiting anymore…..Still, I was absolutely baffled by the night's excitement. 'What had just happened a few hours ago? Were my eyes playing tricks on me now? What could have happened? Oh well, Time to go?' I stood up from the thick bushy heather in which I was settled. My knees were numb after the long seating. I guess I do have a habit of popping my finger to others' businesses when I am not needed. As, I walked forward a peculiar thing happened….

From the distance came a bickering light accompanied by a sound of squealing tires along with the violent banging of metal mixed with the crushing of glass. The noise of metal being bashed over was deafening. It was a flashy German Black Bentley Convertible tumbling over and over, flashing its headlight straight to my eyes. The car flipped so many times and tumbled over and over again, smashing the windows while the glass shattered and the hood crumpled. It was a devastating image. By now, the Bentley was a complete wreck. But the moment it crashed onto the trees, I assumed that no life could be preserved. Bang! Bang! Gun shots echoed again, similar to the ones I had heard just a few hours ago. By now, the car was at absolute rest pierced completely by multiple shots. My mind and heart raced against time. I was doomed. I tried to absorb all of this in. I tried to hide. Yet, my wobbly feet weren't taking me anywhere. I was not in a correct state of mind. I was shocked as everything had happened lighting fast. As the piercing wind slapped my cheek, I came back to this world again. Let alone the black Bentley was stuck, the cliffs were not far behind now and it was stuck amongst the very edge. I couldn't get a glimpse of anyone inside. Yet at least one living person must have been in the car. But I was sure that the victim must have been dead by now as it would be a miracle to survive after this. Not so far away, I could see a lingering shadow getting closer and closer. And without thinking twice, I hid among the trees. I had a good idea of whom the shadow belonged to and believe it or not I was right. It was the same old person, the stranger in the black holding the gun. 'Surely this was an attempted murder', I thought. He continued advancing….I could see him now. Not clearly, yet a mere glimpse of the figure. He wasn't muscularly, more of a timid creature. He approached the Bentley and began to speak, which was the last thing I had expected him to do. What I had expected was more shots and cries for help, a huge tragedy. But, the stranger in black settled down calmly in the bushy heather while still pointing the gun towards the car. Then from an uncivil, brusque tone the stranger began to address someone inside the ruined wreck. I stared without blinking, trying to catch what he was saying….

'Guns aren't like dogs, they don't recognize their owners. If I shoot you'll get shot. So be wise! Give me what I want and everything will be fine. Ignore me, and then….we'll see some fascinating fireworks.' Then he gave a low cruel laugh. He was vulgar. He was a snake. Meanwhile, I was petrified. Up to now I had guessed that years of training had kept me sharp. But I was wrong. I stared. I stood glued to the ground. I wondered what this conversation was about however I didn't understand a word. Yet, my heart started pounding at an increasing rapid pace. The strange in black continued…. 'Be wise! It's a matter in between life and death. You are more likely to get shot being around a guy with a gun. Be smart like you have always been….like your family had always been. It would hurt me to finish you on a personal grudge sweetie.' Well, I didn't actually expect anyone to answer but a small fragile voice spoke. 'Who are you? What do you want?' The voice came from inside the wrecked car. 'Ah! You finally understood girl. What do I want? Well, let me see………The property, the manor and every penny that your family had ever owned, to be true what my family had owned before you all…….'His voice began to tremble and there was a short pause. 'It isn't much right? Be wise, child! Your life depends on this. I really don't want to scratch that charming face of yours, 'he gave a vulnerable laugh. 'Who are you? What are you?' I heard the pleading small voice again. 'Oh! Did I forget to introduce myself dear? Regard to me as the heir of Anderson property. Got it?' The man in black hissed. 'In your dreams!' was the reply but much more steadier this time. I felt the tension between the two. Things were becoming exciting....

'Now, take your time and don't be too frank, I guess it touches your pride. But remember your life or property? Be wise! I am only trying to help. I am a friend.'

'Who on earth are you?' came the answer from inside the ruined car. By now, I was trying to get on my full height to see whoever was inside the wreck. Yet, no one could be seen but someone should definitely be inside. But surely it was a girl, quite young too. Her voice said it all and it seems as if she was hurt. Much talking was done between the two. But neither of them moved a muscle and everything was perfectly still except for the fact that the stranger in black was pointing the gun directly towards the car. I was getting nervous each and every second since I couldn't make out what the conversation was about. I could hear my own heart beat in the same time. I could even hear the nervous breathing of the man in black. I too felt the tension yet I wasn't even involved. The stranger stood up and drew himself to his full height and begun to shake the Bentley which was already struck amongst the edge of the cliff. The car made a strange sound as if to fall off the cliff as it was only a few mere inches away. 'Stop, please have mercy! Please!' plead the voice from inside. 'Help! Save me! Someone, Anyone!' she shrieked. 'My goodness, so sad, there's no one to help you now! Make a decision, your property or your life? It can only be one. Be quick! You, your family should have thought far ahead before bringing this upon yourselves. When I hold a weapon, I am an animal. And now sweetheart, there's no escape and there never will be either. I will regain, what was mine to be all alone.'

'Who on earth are you? Why are you doing this? Have mercy!' pleaded the voice from the car, now trembling as the car was almost fallen across the cliff. She begged. But the answer came as thus. 'Well….let me see, let's just say that fate had wronged me. The mighty, powerful Anderson family….OH, I have had such good memories about them. Those power hungry creatures. I have been simple too in the past, my spring was fresh, and my youth was green. Yet, fate had wronged me. Various circumstances had created this money-hungry evil sinner standing right before you…..No! No! I guess I don't have to explain everything to another Anderson. I have no mercy. I have only one principle. For me money always comes first, second even more money and third much more money. Life is too long and is unfair as it is. It's too late to change anything now…my time has finally come.'

I was carefully hidden as I listened to his short but exciting monologue. His voice had suddenly softened for moment or two. But it didn't last long as he suddenly he raised his voice and how loud it was? The words went like a hypodermic to heart. 'Enough! Past is past. Let's not waste any more time. I will give ten seconds.' As he said this, he threw his arm holding the automatic revolver into the Bentley car. The girl was visible now. I could get one quick glance of her. She was covered in a pool of her very own blood and looked slightly unconscious. The stranger in black held the revolver pointed to her forehead. 'Ten! Nine! Eight...the mighty Andersons had never thought this, had they? Your lives had always been easy, whereas I had always been the one to get hurt and discriminated against....Seven! Six! Five... There is no justice in this cruel world. So....Let's witness what happens to the youngest Anderson. What's your choice? Am I being too nice? Four! Three...We will hit a bulls eye soon, Two!'

'Never ! In your dreams, keep your dirty hands off. Even if it costs a life, my life even then the property shall never by yours' came the feminine voice. 'It won't be a dream anymore. Now, Farewell! Here goes the very last Anderson. Good bye!'....A bullet was coming out now, slowly. Even a seconds delay could have finished her off....By now, I was starting with my ears pierced and eyes wide opened without blinking. I stood where I stood, unable to believe my eyes. How cruel is this world? There were a variety of questions overflowing my brain as if there were a cartoon of birds flying around my skull. I exhaled, inhaled again. But yet, I was frozen stiff. I wanted to charge forward....But my legs restricted me. Sweat poured down my head while the piercing wind slapped my cheek over and over again. Finally, I took a deep, slow breath and even without my conscious, I was proceeding forward... I tip toed, I got closer and closer even though what I was going to do was completely out my will. I just had to do it. It was like fate. I tip toed without making a single sound, not even taking a break to let my breath out. I approached him slowly and now I was behind him....Yet he didn't notice my sudden appearance or maybe just pretending not to. There was a momentary disruption in his firing and I took full advantage. My whole body was paralyzed; I was petrified inside but didn't let it show. He hadn't noticed me but the girl in the car had. She stared suspiciously at my face. Then suddenly, I grabbed his wrist with my right hand. He turned vividly. Surely he hadn't expected me.....The sudden encounter had shocked him, he was astounded. He stared.... without blinding, without even daring to let air out of his nostrils. His posture stiffened. He stood open mouthed while adrenaline slavered from his lips; his brain stuttered for a moment or two….It was like he had forgotten how to breathe. 'What are you?' he muttered. His voice was trembling. Surely his blood had turned into water by now. He was shaking…. He was trembling. He was white as chalk; surely he hadn't expected an Angel to spoil his fun…. He was temporarily incapacitated, unable to comprehend what had just occurred and stood as gormlessly as a guppy. It was my wish to see the man's face but he was cleverly covered in black clothing.

In the momentary disruption….

The girl in the Bentley car struggled to free herself but only rewarded herself with more pain. She was frail and subconscious. She was pinned to the collapsing roof and steering column. I could see her struggling inside. Yet, all her attempts were futile. She was trapped in a metal prison. She struggled….By now; the stranger in black had regained his senses. Our eyes met…He stared. His eyes were as timid as a deer. He didn't seem like a person capable of fighting face to face or eye to eye. How he stared? Several unspoken words were exchanged, not by words but by our eyes. He really despised my appearance. Yet, he couldn't believe his eyes. Then, things started happening rapidly…..The gun was still pointed towards the car aiming the girl's forehead. Yet, the bullet was not coming out; I guessed that he might have run out of them. He struggled like a frantic bird….Suddenly I grabbed his wrist again and twisted it using up all my strength, holding his own gun against his chest. Our eyes met again…...

'Hold it! It is all over! Leave!' I hissed letting out a tone of danger. He looked frightened….Surely, this was not part of the plan. I was still holding this wrist, with the browning automatic revolver pointed to directly his chest. 'It's all over now! Leave! Give up!' When suddenly, there was an explosion. A ball of flame and a fist of grey smoke came from the ruined car. The petrol tank had exploded. There was nothing left in the car now except for a few broken parts which still hanged. It was totally ruined. This grabbed my attention......My heart started to pound rapidly again, unaware of what to do next. 'I must save her life! As I believed in the dignity of life I just had to. The Bentley car was going to fall within a matter of time! The stranger in black broke free from my control, throwing up his forearms like an offensive linesman blocking a defensive block. The car was going to fall! The man held the gun again, pointing towards the girl fighting in between life and death. He was aiming straight towards her forehead. Meanwhile, I was doomed! My feet were tingly. I was in the center of the earth. I guess he still had a few more bullets left in that gun of his. My mind went blank. I couldn't imagine how to save her….The car got stuck again amongst the wild creepers grown along the edge of the cliff….The car or whatever left of it made a peculiar noise as it got entangled among the creepers. There was a pause….The man was ready to shoot, He held the gun pointed towards the girl. Finally, he shot at her. Bang! 'Farewell!' he shouted. 'Good bye! Take care! The very last Anderson.' He had forgotten about me, who stood glued to the ground. Farewell! He screamed. Farewell! The bullet had gone right through the girl's heads. But was she dead? Not yet... she struggled to break free. Yet, nothing could be done. The more she struggled, the more she suffered. The car started to rock….attempting to fall down the cliff. She was glued to the wheel of the wrecked car, screaming for help. She was in the brink of death; only a bit of life was inside her, she dared not to lose it. The stranger in black gave a low cruel laugh which didn't seem to suit him. 'The very last Anderson, farewell!' he screamed and ran. He vanished. He was no longer seen. I was still gazing at the incident. Yet, I made no attempt to catch him. The girl was still struggling. She screamed. She cried and how she cried? Yet, she did not let go of the break. She had not given in. With her broken voice, she cried to me...tears swelling down her cheek. 'Help! Please....Have mercy! Please get me out of here! Please I want to live. Save me, I wanted to die everyday but now I want to live. Please!' she trembled as she said this and went into a coma, unconscious! Sweat poured from her forehead. Her words went in to my heart like a dagger. They really touched me. 'Hold on!' I cried. Do not close your eyes. 'Hold on! Trust me! Wait, do not fall asleep! I am an Angel. I will help!

Hold On! Please!' As I proceeded…. my insides were crumpling on to a ball of silent pain. I wanted to disappear. Yet, I was going to help her. It felt like, I was destined to help her! It was fate. Yet, my mind was still blank, shocked from what I had just witnessed. 'Gosh! What to do? What to do? Still, I had no plan. I scratched my hair, bit my hand and then slapped my own face. The car made a sound again, it was falling…. 'Hold it' I screamed but the girl was in a trauma. She was glued to the seat covered in a pool of blood. The car was falling…. 'Hold on, I am coming!' I screamed on the top of my voice. Yet, she took no notice. The car was almost fallen into the fifty meter drop. Without thinking anymore, I jumped into action. There was no turning back now…either this attempt will kill us both or save us both. I jumped into the car and it shook violently. I was now on the opposite seat next to the girl. I could see that she was young, about my own age or maybe slightly older. The maiden was dressed in a long, white serge frock which was now soaked in blood. Her lips were mangled and her obviously broken down nose drizzled with blood like rain down on a window pane. She looked pale. Yet, she was extremely eye catching and very beautiful with chestnut brown hair waving loosely across her brow. She looked about medium height but I could see nothing more. She was completely ruined. I wasn't sure if she was dead or alive but I had already decided to help her, whoever she was. The car was now shaking even more violently than before. It was all up to luck now. 'Hold it!' I screamed. She was still glued to her seat. She was clutching the steering wheel, her hands wrapped so tightly around it and her feet pushing the brake tightly. 'Let Go!' I cried. 'Trust me and let go! Trust me!' I held on to her hands tightly while giving her an assuring look. 'Trust me! The brake won't help.' I said gently.

'Take your foot off, trust me! I won't let you die. Let's drop the car.' I said in a lighter tone, sounding much more confident than I actually felt. I held onto her hands and tried to lift her. Yet, she was too heavy and fragile to move. Still she was in a trauma. There was only one last thing to do....The car dropped, I wasn't able to save it and it tumbled down the cliff saying its final goodbyes.

Suddenly everything became light. In that instant....My Angel's intuition became active. A pair of glittering wings appeared in my back. I was holding her in my arms. She was still unconscious and I was flying through the air while gathering her in my arms like a stray lamb. We finally landed....everything had happened in the blink of an eye. By the time we had landed, my hands were sore from carrying an adult sized girl. I laid her gently on the think heather. She was in a trauma, in a panic attack or something similar....But alive! I could hear the sound of soft breathing and I was relieved. Thank God! Suddenly, her eyes opened slightly for bit... 'I want to live, save me. I wanted to die everyday but now I want to live Help! Help!' she shrieked. 'You are saved! Thank me later.' But before she could answer, her eyes closed. She became unconscious. She lay calmly in the ground. I could see the gun shot, the bullet had gone through her head, causing it to loose gallons of blood but yet luckily avoiding the fatal area.

The calm descended just after the accident....in that moment the reality of what just happened crashed into my conscious. Then in the distance came a blue flicker and the sound of sirens along with the words written "POLICE" on the first vehicle and the words "AMBULANCE" written in the wagon behind. 'Good Timing!' I thought. By now, the next day had already begun as the darkness was slowly disappearing.

But now, I could feel a particular tingling sensation within my body. The world must have kept flicking its switch because my vision kept flashing from bitter darkness to a binding white light. My head started to spin while the tingling sensation in my body increased, becoming almost unbearable. And then half a second later…. I vanished!

I was been summoned by the Lord God-in-charge!

3. A Trail, a Punishment and another Mission

ithin the next few seconds I could feel myself again. I gazed around and for another second or two I wandered where I was.

'Oh! No.….'

Finally, I returned to my correct state of mind. I could now see that I was standing right outside the gates of paradise, my heavenly realm. And a few meters away….in the distance I could see the blurred image of the Department Of Angel Law And Enforcement. As I stood, gazing at the centuries old magnificent building. I shivered, as though ice had replaced my spine. I had been summoned by the Lord. Surely this wasn't leading to anything good'; I could almost feel it within my bones. The last time   I was summoned, I had to be locked up in a dark, damp cellar for a whole week with nothing except for stale bread and water with the scattering mice for accompany and all that was only for burning Professor Pete's beard off his chin. Of course it was by accident but still god knows what I will get today. 'Oh! What have I got myself into', I cried. 'I haven't done anything that bad right? Oh, damn it!' I have had such good memories of this place that just the reminder gives me goose bumps. I took a deep breath 'Focus IVY! Focus!' Of course, you hadn't done anything that bad, just a few things out of law and order. But surely that was for the betterment of humanity, for the dignity of life, right? No! No! No! What have I got myself in to? I really wished that I could disappear out of sight, out of vision. But I had already being summoned now....'What to do?' Think Ivy! Think! Oh, why does trouble always follow me around?

It's like having a "kick me" sign attached to my back or something. You poor blind fool! Cover your face and be ashamed. Why do you always land yourself on a minefield not knowing when it will explode? There is no one to help you now. Oh! What to do? What to do?' Yet, no matter how I looked into it, what I did was not that bad. I mean it's kind of good, really. It's all for the dignity of life, right? For the peace and prosperity of the land we live in, right? No matter what I said to console myself, I was sure to get punished or maybe even banished or stranded on earth forever. I could see that the promotion I was to get, getting further and further away saying its final goodbyes to me. Of course, that wicked old man would cancel it....I really wish that I could run away now. My mind went blank as I stood staring at the majestic building from afar. 'What to do? What to do?' I tried to cry. Yet, my tears won't spill. I tried to scream yet I couldn't get my voice out. I stood looking far ahead….trying to absorb the bitter truth even though my body wouldn't accept it. By now, I could see that the nighttime darkness had dissolved and a new day had begun. The morning is as assured as the tides and just as unstoppable. I wished that I had a few more hours of blackness. Not to sleep but to prepare for the disciplinary, to pour my thoughts out into a page. Whatever I say, I was sure to be disciplined now that I had been summoned here and surely there was no escape. I sat on the ground with my legs crossed; my head buried within my legs and began to weep. This was not because I was sad but because I wanted to pour my feelings out. How I cried, my tears finally burst forth like water from a dam, spilling down and wetting my face. I heard my own sound like a distressed child, raw from the inside. Perhaps, these tears would wash out my mind. 'Why can't I stop crying? Oh what had I got myself into?' Then suddenly, someone was stroking my hair gently. I recognized the touch at once and as I looked up, the elderly father-like face was facing me straight in the eye. His silky beard overflowed up to his knee and covering his wizened face was a fringe of grey-white hair. He wore a thick black robe and was slightly hunched on the back, leaning heavily on a walking stick. His twinkling bright blue eyes framed by thick bushy eyebrows shone as he threw a warm smile of affection. He calmed me, he always did. 'Save me! Professor Pete, Please! Help me! I will do your chores for a whole year. I promise. Save me! Will he banish me or will I get expelled or….or….'

'Slow down, seriously! Being your chief ages me each day', he said while counting the vast amount of grey hair on his round little head. 'What do you think I am here for? Fun! Being your official guardian until you are twenty one, makes me your representative for the trial,' his voice began to give to echoes all over the place. 'What have you done now? Grow up already! How many times must I repeat myself? DO NOT MEDDLE IN HUMAN AFFAIRS. It's the same every time; you get into trouble and cry for help. Ah….Yet what to do now? 'I doubted whether he was angry or not. 'You have brought his upon yourself, so face it! Just wait until this finishes, I will kill you then!'

'Professor!'

There was nothing affectionate in his voice for sure but yet his expression said it all……He didn't look at the least angry. There was a slight twinkle on his right eye just enough to show that he wasn't mad. His words stumbled as he spoke but his tone was strong, clear and distinctly upper classes like a sergeant major.

'Professor, I'….

'You didn't think this far, Ah great…But what did you expect? I'm not able to save you this time. It's completely out of my hands. Solve it yourself. You've bought this upon yourself,' he said. 'Professor, help me! I promise that I won't let you down. Just this once, I am begging you….Please! Will I….get, you know….'

'What!'

'Banished or something like that or something similar….'

'Well, do not ask me….I cannot tell. It is totally out of my control. Your past is not that clean either, remember……' he said pointing towards the burned ends of his silvery beard.

'Oh….Yeah but….Did I really do something that bad? I mean dignity of life. That is what I am talking about.' After this, his tone suddenly lightened. Becoming not so much distant anymore… 'So, Ivy what exactly happened? You didn't do anything rash, did you?' I poured out my story, adding a few bits along the way to make it sound interesting and without even stopping to breathe….much to my own relief Professor Pete listened without any hesitation. 'You don't spare your breath do you?' he said. 'What?' I exclaimed. 'Just to make you laugh, but I bet it wasn't very funny right?' he answered. 'Thanks Professor …'

'So, Child….Let's get to the point shall we? Did Miss Turner survive' 'Who?' I asked. 'Miss Turner, the girl you saved', he said. 'Ah….So that's her name. Well, I am not sure, Professor.

But I guess' I said much more confidently now that I have professor by my side. 'Well, she did....in the hospital now, unconscious yet alive! Thanks to a certain someone. Listen, Ivy....my child even if the whole world looks down on you and point their fingers at you. If what you did is true, honest and with a pure heart. You will always be rewarded. It might take a year, a month or a day' I listened in silently to his inspiring words. 'Thanks....Professor....Thanks a lot. At least you understand me.'

'No, I don't Ivy. I'm just trying to be a responsible guardian. I never cared for you, just showing off my charm.' Yet, there was the habitual twinkle in his eye. And I smiled. 'I almost forgot....This conversation went a bit too far, Here.' he said. And with his shaky hands he held out a script. 'Read it thoroughly, See you soon. Be on time. Do not be late!' and he left, limping as he went....I was left alone to my thoughts. Professor Pete....was surely a good sort; He had a heart of pure gold, whatever, people said about him. I opened the script and it stated thus.....

Dear Miss Ivy Splencer,

This is an official warning under the Angelic low No 2452 Decree no 5432 for the use of Angel intuition. (Mode Used-wings) in front of a human and under Angelic low 2562 decree no 5582 for meddling in human affairs.

<u>The Disciplinary Hearing</u>

Name   :Elizabeth Ivy Splencer

Age   :Twenty Years.

Blood group   :O positive

Zodiac Sign   :Pisces

Position   :Junior Guardian Angel

Role   :In-charge of half dead humans

Official Guardian   :God-in-charge   Honorable Professor Pete Arnold Fransaic Jefferson (Chief)

Venue   :Department of Angel Law and Enforcement, the heavenly realm

Life of an Angel

Date	:16th July 1990
Time	:6.00am-9.00 am (Can be varied)
Participants will be	:Elizabeth Ivy Splencer and God-in-charge Honorable Professor Pete Arnold Fransaic Jefferson (Representative)
Jury	:Dorothy Schweitzer (Interrogator), Robinson William Hughes (Interrogator), Susan Amelia Thomas (Interrogator), Robert Andrews (Court scribe)
Judge:	:God in change of the Angel World. Honorable Majesty the great, his Highness Lord Professor Emanuel Wulfric Brian Hamilton
Significance	:Disciplinary hearing for junior guardian Angel Elizabeth Ivy Splencer
Description	:We regret to inform you that you will be expected at the Department of Angel Law and Enforcement, the heavily realm twenty three minutes and fifteen seconds before the above mentioned time. You are to bring your representative (God In charge/Official Guardian) along with you. Your participation is highly is highly appreciated. Your fullest cooperation is needed.

Yours sincerely
Senior Secretary.
   (Department of Angel Law and Enforcement, Heavenly realm)

I read it out over and over again until each and each every word got memorized within my head. Regardless, how much I stared at the paper, nothing changed. And as the distant clock tower struck 5.00, there was not much time left either. The hearing was to be started soon and in a matter of time I'll be facing him while having a heart to heart time with the 'Dread Judge'. My legs were numb and I did not want to move. I just wanted to get dissolved in the shadows. Life is just so unfair! I mean, what is the big deal of saving a life. Time was flying and I needed to make haste, nothing could be changed now. I did not have much of a choice anyway. Along the way, my head pounded rapidly and I could hear it thudding while I broke into sweat. By now, I could feel the sweat bending down on my forward but yet I wanted to look confident without giving away the fact that I was scared to death. So I advanced forward, taking a few small steps at a time. And without noticing, I found myself standing right in front of a strongly built castle, extended over the centuries. Its gold domed towers gave it a picturesque look. My heart leapt as I gazed up at the sight. As it stood on the rugged slope, trees surrounded it. I had been so lost, my head buzzing with the possibilities that I might be banished from my world that I was surprised to see how far I had come and that the two mile walk didn't seem much. 'You can do this! You got this! Go for it girl! Come on!' I took a few more slight steps forward and seconds later the gigantic Iron Gate loomed in front of me. I debated for a while whether to enter or not. 'It's now or never!'

It hadn't been that long since I was last here and nothing had seemed to change at all. It was grand as usual. The whole department was carpeted with indigo material with elaborated gold designs, draped with tapestries and dark clothing making the whole place look regal. It was a huge crowded place with various angels of different categories engaged in their own fields of work. However, it was dimly lit that the inky darkness engulfed the frail light diminishing all the happiness that had risen with the sun. I tried looking for Professor Pete yet he couldn't be seen anywhere....'Maybe, he was already seated in the disciplinary council....'and I proceeded forward; my poor heart began to race again. The cold damp air wrapped around me like a heavy coat of chain mail as I descended the spiral staircase to the disciplinary room for guardian Angles. The absence of flaming torches created a dimness giving the impression of twilight despite the heat and brilliance of the early July morning. My brain felt full of static like an old television set that had lost its signal. A part of me was screaming to turn around, how badly I wanted to disappear but I didn't dare to. I must face this. My past, present and future as an Angel depends solely on this hearing. I could feel the tension boiling inside my body much more than ever now. I was really close to the disciplinary room; it was just a few inches away and definitely there's no turning back. My heart was racing now....I could feel the sweat bending down on my forehead as I walked around the corner....Finally; the great massive crimson metal door confronted me. I took a step closer but then again paused. 'The Stress, Oh.... My!' This was the very last barrier that separated me and the disciplinary room. The moment I open this, things will start happening. My future depended on this. I took another step back. I really wanted to vanish. 'Hold yourself together Ivy, Take it easy!' I took another step back and silently glared into its thick panel, the melancholic feeling inside me was almost absolutely unbearable But, What to do? I had bought this upon myself, didn't I? I stood shaking, my feet were still numb. I glared at the door, it was almost time....'I had to do it, Okay! Let's go, now or never!' I pulled up the courage and in the count of three, one.... I stretched my hand Two.... I twisted the door nob. Then, I pushed it with the point of my finger nails and the heavy iron-bound door swung open. I could see several eyes staring down at me as I proceeded. Yet, I tried to avoid eye-contact as much as possible. I was just too nervous....Walking into the room, I took in my breath sharply. I was a soldier entering a battlefield and just stepping into the room made my breathing rapid and shallow; while my heart threatened to burst from its rib case. I could feel my pulse pounding. Yet, I wanted to seem as confident as I could.....I tried to straighten my face and look around. I had just entered an enormous crowded place with low ceilings, a roof of gray slate, walls of polished marble stone and highly polished dark wooden floor. In the back of the room was a marble fireplace big as a sepulcher. Further more, there were serried rows of benches raised in all levels around the ground, all positioned so that they could have a clear view of the high stool in the center of the room in which the person to be disciplined is to be seated. Just facing it was a throne carved of rich, fine oak crested with shimmering jewels and numerous foams of decorative materials giving it a magnificent heavenly look which was to be seated by the Honorable Majesty Lord his highness. As I went forward ...I could see that many were staring, whispering certain things about me or at least I imagined about me. Yet, Professor Pete wasn't to be seen anywhere. I got tensed. 'Where on earth could this old man be?' He was to be my official representative yet I couldn't catch sight of him anywhere. The heavy iron-bounded door on the left side swung open and everyone got to their feet, the silence prevailed...... In came a flawless figure gleaming with pride wearing a long loose–fitting black silk robe. His existence was universal....'Honorable Majesty Lord Professor Emanuel Wulfric Brian Hamilton has arrived....Let the disciplinary commence.' It was starting, where was this dumb professor?

Dorothy Sciewtzer (Interrogator): 'The disciplinary hearing of Junior Guardian Angel Miss Elizabeth Ivy Splencer, commencing on the Sixteenth of July 1990 at the Department of Angel law and Enforcement, Heavenly realm. May the Jury be seated......May everyone be seated'....... (There was a pause) I was nervous...... I was as tensed as a long-tailed cat in a room of rocking chairs. But where was Professor? Still, it was a relief to finally sink into my stood, embarrassing as it was. I was glad as my legs were shaking and I was quite afraid of falling any second. 'But where was that old coot, Where on earth was he? He did say that he would come ... Didn't he?'

Interrogator: - 'The time is 6.00 am and the expected time to end is 9.00am. May the court be silent!'

The silence was prevailed.......

I stayed......seated on the high stood in the middle of the room facing the 'Dread Judge'. I broke into sweat again yet trying to keep my face as straight as possible. My heart pounded non-stop.....And my hands began to feel clammy against my bouncing knee. Life is just so unfair, what have I done to reserve this and where was Professor Pete? My poor heart jumped into my mouth....The tension was all around the room. Basically, I needed some backup yet Professor Pete couldn't be seen anywhere....Had I been backstabbed by my one and only companion, guardian and teacher? I felt a strong sense of isolation....

Interrogator : 'Miss Spencer, As you have already received the official warning under the Angelic law No. 2452, Decree No : 5432 for the use of Angel Intuition (wings) in front of a human and Under Angelic law No : 2562 Decree No : 5582 for the Meddling of Human Affairs ,your presence have been required at a disciplinary hearing, any objections?'

'Well, yeah....You see.' (But I got ignored)

Interrogator: 'Let's continue, Shall we? Junior Guardian Angel, Miss Elizabeth Ivy Splencer is currently residing at No. 562 555, the balcony in Heavenly realm. She is Junior to Honorable Professor Pete Arnold Fransaic....' Suddenly, the sound of thudding footsteps could be heard advancing towards the room, it was getting louder and louder. And the door swung open....In came Professor Pete...... I breathed relief, 'That old man! He always made his appearances at the most unusual times......'by now, everyone was staring at the professor, yet he came forward in his usual calm manner and his face with no expressions. He gave a small low bow as if nothing had happened. 'What's going on?' exclaimed the lord. 'Pardon me Brian, lost track of time, sorry about that. I was having a blast with me cup of pine needle tea with whipped cream and a cherry on top and kind of thought that it'll be 6.00 pm and not am. Sorry about that again. Pardon me, Brian but may I take me seat.' (Informal) By now, everyone was staring at the Professor now without blinking....The great Lord waved a hand of dismissal and Professor Pete took his seat among the Jury without a care in the world. 'What a man!' I forgot my own troubles for a moment or two. 'Professor sure was something remarkable, what a nerve he had!'

'Continue!' ordered the Lord

Interrogator: - 'As I was saying....She is Junior to Honorable Professor Pete Arnold Fransaic Jefferson. Any objections.... (No one spoke)

I tried to put in a few words, 'Well, Yeah you see....' (But got ignored again)

Interrogator: - 'On the midnight of the15[th] July, 1990 while Miss. Splencer was on duty in the Argurum Shrubbery. She is said to have witnessed an attempted murder in which Miss. Rachel Ingramme Anderson Turner, No. 24/7 Anderson Manor, near Plywood was the victim. The incident had been confirmed and had happened at 12.30 pm. According to all the evidences identified so far, Miss.Splencer had thoughtlessly gotten involved in this incident and was able to preserve the life of Miss. Turner on the same day. By now, Miss. Turner is getting treated at St. Maureen's private hospital, close to Plywood in the Intensive Care Unit, Unconscious but alive. Today we regret to inform that Miss. Splencer had used her Angel intuition (wings) in front of Miss. Turner and thus going against the Angelic law No. 2452, Decree No: 5432. Meanwhile, she too has gone against the Angelic law No: 2562 Decree No: 5582 for the Meddling of Human Affairs which was implemented from the 2nd of September 1935. Consequently, My Lord, Junior Guardian Angel Elizabeth Ivy Splencer is to be banished from this world or on the other hand disciplined appropriated according to the laws of our world.' By now, I was sitting on the stool my heart pounding faster than ever. I was petrified....I really was in a tight situation.

'Interesting, really interesting,' said the Lord. His mouth forming a rigid grimace, with arms folded tightly across his broad chest while tapping his foot furiously. 'Interesting, really interesting, Miss Splencer....As I can remember....You had a troubled past, right?'

'Yes, My Lord. I beg your pardon but I sincerely hope that my past actions would not be considered in a day like today.'

'It's definitely like you Miss Splencer, to go on causing trouble.' But before he could continue a man from the Jury shouted, 'She was a menace as a stripling. Oh, yeah I could remember her academy days'....

'Silence!' shouted the Lord. 'The disciplinary will commence.... Miss Splencer's official guardian will now start speaking.....' Professor Pete advanced, limping as he came while leaning ever so heavily on his poor walking stick. He looked so calm, nothing disturbed him. I tried to catch his eye. Yet, he wasn't looking anywhere. He looked straight-forward and totally determined as if he had the whole world in his arms.

'Start, Professor......'

Professor Pete....started in his steady, strong and distinctly upper class voice which echoed throughout the room, 'Requesting permission to speak my Lord' he asked humbly. 'Permission granted you may start....'echoed the expected answer. 'I Pete Arnold Fransaic Jefferson, God-in charge and Official Guardian of Junior Guardian Angel Miss. Elizabeth Ivy Splencer until the Fourth of July, 1991 have totally agreed towards all charges against her and insists that she shall be punished accordingly for her thoughtless actions according to the Angel Law and Order. Yet, I as her senior and official guardian requests that she shall not be banished but instead, be given a much fairer punishment. Wrong she may be, but her actions were true, honorable and pure alas she should be highly regarded for that. Yet, she should be punished. If, I may suggest....She should be locked in the cellar for 200 days and no nights with only bread and water.'

'The court be silent! We shall attend to your story after a break of 2 hours, 20 minutes and 9 and a quarter seconds. Dismissed'....

By now, I had regained my confidence. I was totally freaked out. But....I guess not so much now. It was fifty percent. 'No! I won't get banished, not today at least. The cellar punishment was much better, difficult though it was.'

'Professor' I called as he came towards me. 'Better,' he asked. 'A lot better, Thanks!' I answered. 'Be patient Ivy, you poor child. Everything is going to be just fine, difficult but fine!' he said. 'Thanks, Professor whoa....You did give me a shock though.'

'You don't know me well enough child; I am always in the correct place at the correct time. Times almost up, better get going now. And.... one last advice, if they ever question be sure to make the explanation as clear as mud....That's my trick by the way.'

'Thanks a bunch Professor,' I remarked. 'There you go kiddo. Good luck out there'.

2 hours, 20 minutes and 9 and a quarter seconds later;

Interrogator: - 'The court remain silent! (The silent prevailed) Everybody remain seated!'

Lord: -'Taking all the facts into consideration, considering each and every decree we have reached a conclusion .....'

'The disciplinary action taken against Junior Guardian Angel Elizabeth Ivy Splencer will be announced shortly'........

Interrogator((Robinson William Hughs) ;- 'The punishment against Miss. Splencer will be that she will be deployed to the earth for a mission of three months, 2190.002 hours commencing from the 17th July,1990 starting from 9.55 am. Her past, present and future will solely depend on this so she is expected to do her best within this time period. 'I was listening to all this with both my ears pierced. But why is it always me? I couldn't believe my ears. This was unjust. How could they do this to me? Darn it! What had I done that wrong to deserve this?

Interrogator; - 'After the near-fatal accident, the victim Miss Rachel Ingramme Turner had been saved. Yet......the incident had made her differently abled and also a change in her character could be observed as she had suffered brain damage. The poor girl has now developed a cold, vulgar and insolent behavior which seems to clash from her original self. So, Miss Elizabeth Ivy Splencer's duty will be to get deployed to the earth and remain there until Miss. Turner opens up to her. You will be her guide, her eye and her friend. Until she does open up to you, you will stay there.....Seek you own food, shelter as you are not permitted to take anything, absolutely anything from the heavenly realm except for your good will and the currently worn clothing. 'But ... Wait!'(Yet, I got ignored again)

'As of now, from sixteenth July, 1990 9.55am you are human! All powers you had both as an angel, a guardian angel and as a member of the heavenly realm will disappear this day forth. The moment you step out of the heavenly realm, they will only be a memory within that time. You will give a daily report in the dawn of each day for 3 months to your God-in charge Honorable Professor Pete

Arnold Fransaic Jefferson and this is expected to be carried out regularly. Success, in this mission and you'll return back....A Failure; you will be stranded on the Earth forever .Be wise! You life depends on this....May this mission benefit us all and return with Victory!'

The great Lord who had been silent for all this time finally spoke up, 'Miss. Splencer will now take the oath. 'Up to now, I've been glued to my stool, unable to imagine what could happen next.....I was bewildered.....Various thoughts scattered around my head. Several unanswered questions flew around my head. I felt like I was walking on eggshells. 'Miss. Spencer, The oath,' said the mighty lord. 'What!' I inquired. 'The oath if you may' came the hallow voice. 'Sorry sir, what?' I asked again. 'The oath, Miss.Splencer'...... 'Beg your pardon, Sorry my lord.' As I stood up my legs tingled. I couldn't still believe what was happening. Yet, I outstretched one of my hands and began thus......

'I've been given permission as an Angel, thus I faithfully bow to give my life to serve humanity, the selfish mankind. Their souls will be my utmost priority. I will faithfully carry out my duties towards my home the heavenly realm and my duties as an Angel while faithfully concealing my identity. Regardless of gender, ethnicity, religion, skin color and economic status I will carry out my duties with equality. I will use my training humanely even when I am under threat or in the brink of death. I Junior Guardian Angel Elizabeth Ivy Splencer, age 20 born on the 4th of July 1970 hereby take this oath on my account and behalf of my Angel honor! DIGNITY OF LIFE! Thank you'.... I said sounding much more confident than I truly felt.

'She is dismissed!' said the mighty Lord.

Everything was finished! Finally! But...What would happen next? I just couldn't imagine what to do next. Why does it always have to be me! Oh, Why....Oh why....Oh why? I was not frightened enough to give me butterflies in my stomach but it did make me a little apprehensive. By now, Professor Pete too had come out. I ran toward him......

'Save me Professor! Save me! What can I do next?'

'What did you expect?' But soon his tone smoothened. 'Ivy, listen my child! An Angel isn't made in a day. Don't think that our life is a featherbed. It takes years of perseverance, discipline and thousands of missions to earn the coveted title of Ministering Angel. Be patient, my child. Keep in mind that your past, present and future depends solely on this. It's not something you could run away from....Your light-hearted approach to life won't work anymore....Grow up! Be mature! Certainly, you are not a child anymore. Your face seemed to have age a decade in the past few hours and I hope you have too,' his voice was enough to give me a bit of warmth. 'Thanks a million Professor, I wish I could be like you too but I haven't done anything wrong have I?   To deserve all this......' 'You have done nothing wrong. Your actions were pure and that's all that matters. You did right, my child even though, we all are too self-centered to accept it....Now remember be true, avoid hard work then all will be well. Don't give up just because you don't know what to do. Stay strong! 'These words went like a dagger to my heart's core; they were so true, so real and yet so wise. At least one person in this world believed me and it meant a lot to me. Those words were like a shower of rain after a draught. 'Thanks Professor for everything. Goodbye Sir! ....'

'Ivy, Wait here...... Keep this with you' and he held out his hand and placed a yellow gold chain on my hand. 'Keep this with you....Use it in the time of need. One wish! That's all it holds. Use it wisely! I am not exactly supposed to give you this but remember there should be an exception to every rule.'

'Thanks Professor....I really mean it. Goodbye Sir! Goodbye my home! I will return with victory! Goodbye, Fighting!'

(An old chapter of my life had just closed and a new one opening ....)

4. The Quest, a Dreadful Journey

ADistant church clock struck ten as I passed it. As of now, The 'Human Elizabeth Ivy Splencer' was born....I was on a road, the road which carried me towards my mission. To somewhere call 'Anderson Manor' or 'Andrews Manor', I wasn't really sure what it was called. Walking felt blissful, the two worlds that an Angel and a human live were clearly different whether it's good destiny or bad destiny its 'Two Worlds.' I had miles to go, thousands and thousands of miles. The path ahead gleamed like a shimmering silver white ribbon inviting me to step on it and proceed forward. The day was postcard perfect. The skies were an unbroken backdrop of blue....I walked down the streets under the gold but pale broad bar of sunlight that warmed my skin. The sunlight came in form of woven strands free and united, flowing into the day it reveals and solidifies while the friendly honey-comb yellow ball, the glowing medallion of the sky promised more heat as the day progresses. The sky was baby-blue, not psychedelic candy blue nor washed out grey, there were puffs of radiant joy ready to disperse into the wind and travel into this earth. I stopped, closed my eyes as I breathed in the fresh air. 'Blue skies, no ghastly wind plus the perfect temperature....What more could I ever want? Perfection! It was just too good for my long quest to the Manor....But what happens after?' They wouldn't just take me in anyway. I was a stranger, a total stranger....I couldn't even compensate for anything as I had nothing except, of course for what I currently wore. I had no money! I had nothing left in the world. Despite the magnificent scenery, a melancholic feeling began to surround me. Whatever happens who would know? Who would even care? It's not like I belonged to someone. I could feel the fear underneath my chest growling. Yet, for one second I hadn't regretted my actions that night. What I had done was right, It was pure and with a good heart. Still, I could feel the draining of color from my face while my stomach churned continuously. But I overcame it while the fear went away and settled somewhere deep inside my body, sitting like an angry ball of fire trying to propel towards myself anytime I try to loosen the grip. 'Enough!' I said to myself. 'We'll get to that later. And now, let's enjoy this spectacular day. 'It was a splendid midsummer day, very hot. Skies were azure and radiant while being bright and serene at the same time, accompanied by the placid sunshine. Sweet briar and jasmine, pinks and roses yielded their summer fragrance along with the fresh breeze.

In the same moment, the primroses had made their own wealth on the ground beneath. I proceeded; taking short breaks along the way to admire this illumination which gives vivacious hues to the world of living art. I wondered how many hues of green my eyes were witnessing. I felt as light as a feather. 'Providence was too good to be true!' I closed my eyes allowing the rays to sink into my skin, feeling the warmth of the brilliant rays on my face. I stretched my arms, fingers towards the sun feeling the light, breathing the air and slowly began to dance. I was a part of it; I was quite lost in nature's spectacular glory. It was a wonderful sight. The grass was a soft green that almost had a hit of blue while the trees are dancing ladies in fabulous dresses of green, much more brilliant than any designer craft. They waved their hands at me and I waved back. They were being choreographed by the now blowing wind. This is life! I forgot all my

worries for a minute or two even though I was actually in a very tight situation. I continued to admire the beauty....As I advanced further; I could experience the laughter of our winged friends crying to one another in a language which I could never understand even if I tried. Music filled my ears. If by chance, their music was visible it would be soft petals falling like rain. I felt them as auditory smiles and expressions of joy. My spirits lifted up into the sky and felt as if I was walking up on a cloud of joy. I guess human life isn't all that bad, right? The melodious chorus had hydrated my parched soul. Breathtaking! Much to my own grief the happiness didn't last long, it was only short-lived.....

Eight hours later,

The journey continued, far it was. Yet a destination couldn't still be seen. I walked and walked until at last my feet were sore. I had almost enough by now, spending several torturous hours walking on foot. There was nothing to boost up my spirits. I felt like a worn out shoe. My stomach growled, reminding that I hadn't had anything for nearly three whole days while my head felt lighter than usual as If someone had pulled out my brains. Yet, I had no money at least to buy myself something to chew. My body needed to rest, this was torture. This was a living hell. Yet my mind needed to move. I was tired, hungry too. I hadn't the time to stop, time was ticking and I still hadn't come half of the distance to Andrews Manor or whatever it was called. It was a very long walk....but sleep was definitely out of the question. Fifteen hours later; I was drained. I reached a small town called Heather wood and from there I reached Radcliff. By now, I had almost traveled a distance of seventy miles on foot. I didn't dare to take a break but continued.... As I pass the small towns, I was like a waif among the strangers. My stomach growled again as I felt the smell of freshly baked bread rolls coming from inside the little shops planted along the roadside. I was ravenous, I was totally **famished!** I really wanted to sink my teeth into a decent meal; I couldn't remember the last day in which I had one. I couldn't resist the urge anymore. My stomach rumbled again, much ferociously this time but I tried to cover it with my hands. I felt weak now. The more I tried to resist the pain….the harder it got. Finally, with much hesitation I decided to sell my coat, my only source of warmth so as to get food. I went into a little shop with the notice outside 'Barley's shop, best prices offered for old clothes.' There was a hairy young lad inside. 'Gosh! He snarled. 'What do you want? Grr!'he questioned. 'Sir, may I exchange this clothing for a bit of food,' I asked. 'Some cheese and bread would do just fine, 'I added.

'My goodness, Garr!' said the lad. 'No! Bread and water,' he said and I agreed. But he didn't want to give me any food. I waited for a whole hour and then at last he handed me a parcel covered in opaque colored clothing. But I couldn't open the parcel there as the lad wanted to kick me out as soon as possible. But I thanked him gruffly and went out. I opened the parcel. I was shocked! It was **empty! Except for a few pieces of decayed** wood, there was no food. I had no warm clothing either, nothing! And my destination was no where near. I continued....I walked passing several towns, villages and gloomy forests. Finally, I reached a dark and eerie part of a wood. I couldn't continue any longer. I was hungry and my feet were sore. I was hungry as a bear in spring. I starved to death. If there was only some way to get a bite of something at least eatable....Everything was hard now. I felt the difficulty to move and my limbs were shaky. By now, I was genuinely afraid that I might die of hunger. Hours passed….I walked and walked….days passed….More hours went by yet I could see no destination and no Anderson Manor either. It was my seventeenth day now, I am weak. I opened my mouth. Yet, I was too weak to cry. My body so badly needed rest yet my mind needed to move. On top of all this, my throat felt drier than the baked summer sun. The evening slowly droned on. By now, even my saliva was thick like wallpaper paste. My throat felt parched and my skin was like it had been extracted and laid out in the scorching sun to dry. I felt tormented. My head banged and throbbed. I felt as if energy was being constantly drained out of me as though I'm leaking electricity. I felt slightly out of focus. I thought I would black out soon while the ringing sensation in my throat grew more and more. I continued advancing even though I couldn't move a muscle, they were stiff. It felt like every muscle was slowly giving away into gravity. I was a walking zombie, dead inside but subconsciously awake. 'Chaos was always a friend of mine!' My body was begging for rest....Yet, I ignored. I continued....I was half dead now, my life was slowly draining and I felt it. I hadn't eaten nor slept for nearly five days now. It was a miracle that I was still alive. I was famished, weak and even my legs felt empty. I had a black hole instead of a stomach now. I was unable to last longer....My sight blurred due to the scorching heat while making my poor eyes watery and forcing me to witness imaginary images. I could now see an imaginary house in front; twice I had been fooled this way. My breath became ragged and the air moved sluggishly over my mouth. I felt like a dying fish, struggling when taken out of the ocean. I proceeded, taking small steps as I advanced.... 'Someone help! Anyone! Please help!' I muttered. My body felt heavy, my legs wobbled, my skin became as pale as my eyes and my face turned stony while my brain stopped sending signals to the muscle cells. I was dying inside and it was extremely painful. My vision went fuzzy and I was light headed for a minute or so ...Then suddenly, I could see a house somewhat similar to a castle. It was like an old man standing on top of a cliff. But was this real! Yet, it seemed so....But as I tried to run...was it just me or was it getting further and further away.

In this instant, I couldn't feel anything. I cried in agony....The whole world went back! Then with one step backward, I fell! I crumpled like a puppet suddenly being released from his string. And there I laid....Fallen in the dirt as still as a corpse!

I was lying in the doorstep of death....

5. Anderson Manor and the Beginning of a New Life

'I Was not alone but in an unknown road, I was lost. I was close to death and looked pale. But there was another girl, alongside with me. But that wasn't me. I was only a baby, nineteen years younger. It was a younger version of myself but the baby was me, I was sure of it. There was another child, a girl about my own age with chestnut colored hair and a pale face. We were not strong enough to stay together. The other baby was drifting further and further away into an unknown path. I was crying, begging for us to remain together but she was disappearing and I was left all alone in the howling wind, God of Death asking me to come to him. I was alone!'

The pale gold lemony flecked rhomboids of the sunlight had filled the entire room creating a warm sensation like a flamboyant guest, not waiting for an invitation.

It was morning, and outside the artistic gold sun had risen like a whining baby throwing a beacon of light rays thickly through the mullioned panes of glass, illuminating the darkened room while bathing the black and white tiled floor in a crisscross of iridescent color.

The bright morning sun had kissed me awake. Yet, my eyes were still shut as I soaked in the warmth of my thick covers burrowing myself into the warm, soft sheets. Waking up surely wasn't easy! The warm glow was mesmerizing. I felt hot underneath the covers. Soon, I stood up straight as I could no longer bare the gentle touch of sunlight on my skin. My eyelids flickered open....I rubbed away the remainders of sleep from my eyes, stretched my arms above my head and gave out a big yawn. I had just risen from a heavy slumber….

I am awake; slowly the fatigue of the dreadful journey was seeping out of me. My insides were crumpled in a ball of silent pain. Where am I? Slowly and reluctantly, I uncovered my face. I blinked, closed my eyes and blinked again. Where was I? Much to my own surprise I was laying on top of a huge decorated bed with an elaborated Mahogany headboard. Where am I? My heart was pounding like crazy. What was happening? I half wondered if I was still dreaming….Nope! That wasn't it either, I was awake for sure, perhaps more fully awaken than I had ever been before....Am I still alive? Didn't I just die? My heart was still pounding, skipping two or three beats along the way. My mind was empty. How come I am still alive? I had to run my hands all over my body to check if I was all there, Hands...Check! Legs...Check!

Hair...Check! Nose...Check! I guess I was myself after all. Ok now, let's get this straight shall we? Where am I? What had just happened? I tried to trouble my brain to get a mere idea about what had just happened. Yet, the only things inside were a couple of slightly blurred and completely blurred images. All I could remember was fainting in the middle of nowhere. I was rattled. What was this strange place? Did someone rescue me? Questions of varied types flooded my brain. What was going on here? My heart skipped another beat as I glanced around the room I was in. It was a solitary place, quite dreary. Yet, very handsome, grand and stately with navy-blue walls thickly paneled with walnut and an incredibly high ceiling, hanging down it was an ornate chandelier. I wandered where I was? I was little used to grandeur. So, this kind of felt awkward. I looked around a bit more, still seated on top of my bed. It was the most beautiful room I had ever seen, quite different from the quarters of the junior guardian angels back at the heavenly realm. I focused my eyes beyond the room with its yellow–gold carpets which were embroidered with images of garlands of flowers, the sparkling glass ornaments of bohemian glass and the crimson couches and chairs. The walls were covered with oil paintings of old–bearded men in tunics and ruffs while a handsome, long, polished wooden table stood in the distant corner of the room. For a moment or two, I was absorbed in a world of my own thoughts….Suddenly; I could hear two sets of footsteps coming towards the room. One was heavy and one light. My heart suddenly jumped into my mouth, I could hear someone twisting the door knob. I didn't want to face anyone just yet. The great oak door swung open….I burrowed my weak figure into the warm soft sheets. In came a man...accompanied by a lady who would probably have been the maid or a housekeeper or anyone similar. I guess he had seen me already as he addressed me…. 'I guess you have woken up, Ma'am finally! We were worried sick about you.' I felt a bit embarrassed at first….My cheeks grew a bit red but I tried to sit up straight as I could and arrange my hair a bit which was quite messy, don't ask!

'Well…oh….excuse me….' I suddenly exclaimed not knowing what to say. He smiled gently. 'We are glad you have woken up, Ma'am.'

'OH….that, what happened….? Where am I? What's this place?'

'I guess you are still in shock... But first things first! May I introduce myself, Sir Lloyd Balleywick, official butler and caretaker of the great Anderson manor at your service,' the man said in a husky yet orotund voice which seemed mysteriously familiar. 'I….so this is Anderson manor, Ah! What had happened what's all this?' 'That's what we should be asking you. But first things first introductions later....' he said his voice suddenly turning official and business–like. He raised his hand and gave a sign from his fingers to the lady still standing outside the great oak door, silently waiting as a statue until her presence was required. 'Mrs. Ophelia, if you please.' he added and the lady came inside and began filling a small round basin in the far left corner of the room. 'Ma'am you'd better change your clothing, let's resume our conversation again....later. Ok then, wish you a bright, pleasant day,' he said making a movement of dismissal with his hand and turning around to leave. 'Wait! Mr. Butler, what happened? Where am I?' He smiled but didn't turn back as if he didn't hear my question. 'Wait! Mister pleases what happened, wait! How long have I been here?' I asked again trying to be as polite as I could. 'Four days!' was the reply as the door creaked and shut close with a thud. I examined him as he went out…gliding as he did, the butler Mr. Lloyd seemed like a middle aged man about forty five, his face white as a sheet. Yet, stern with a severe expression and a frown across his brow, the rest he seemed to be about medium height. He was high shouldered, his clothes were well-brushed and he wore a block frock coat along with a black tie and had red hair cut very short. He looked a gentleman, quiet that at first glance I mistook him for the owner or master of this place. I didn't want to like him yet the gentleness in his manner, despite the roughness seemed to put me at ease. There was a strange oddity in the air as he spoke like he wasn't actually meaning what he said, there was deep sadness in the voice as he spoke. I really didn't want to like him but in this moment I did!

I was still seated in my warm bed cross legged while the thick navy blue covers covered part of my body. Waking up surely wasn't easy as I wanted to stick glued to the bed and stay there forever without facing the world. My body was aching all over which was something I never felt as an angel, I guess I was completely human now. It surely was harsh. Let's get this straight now, shall we? He did say that this is the great "Anderson manor" didn't he? It means this is Anderson manor, my destination right? So if he was only the butler there must be a master or mistress right? Was it the person whom I had just saved a few days ago? Surely, this was a huge place for one young girl like her. Why couldn't I remember anything that happened that night! You poor thing, you idiot! But for gods sake what next!

I must have been like a nutcase striking myself and jabbering to myself that when I finally came to my senses I could see that the lady that had come in with Mister, I mean the butler was staring at me as if I was the most bizarre thing in the world. Just seeing her expression, I could imagine what she was anticipating deep down in her mind. Surely, she was thinking if I was an alien from another planet or something. I tried to straighten up, arrange myself and tried to get down from my bed. I felt stiff, I had just roused from a heavy slumber after four days, just imagine. My ragged clothes felt damp, shabby and on top of that they were dirty and torn after the long walk. 'Your basin is ready ma'am,' called out the lady from the corner of the room. It was the first time she had spoken after coming in here. 'Thanks….Ms.….'

'Call me Ophelia Ma'am,' she said. My lungs and heart expanded as I yawned. I stepped out of the bed….My legs felt shaky as they hadn't touched the ground for several days. I precariously took a step forward, slowly and reluctantly. 'Better change into something else ma'am, you have a look out of this world….'

came the voice from the corner of the room. Much more of a whisper as if she was afraid of waking up the dead. I smiled, it was honest and I knew it. I advanced forward but not towards the basin but towards the rectangular glass window and gazed out. The radiant sun was shining in the sky like a vast ball of fire scattering its white rays throughout the valley beneath. The few large white clouds lingering in the pale, washed out blue sky was a magnificent sight. A few hills had risen out in the horizon and a bit further away a meadow with scraggly trees and bushes. And to the further west was a quite lonely spot, a place which was like where the heavens and the earth met. 'What is that Mrs. Ophelia', I asked pointing towards the west. The lady came towards me but she didn't look pleased....Yet she answered.... 'Now, ma'am your bath is getting cold.' 'Okay, but what's that?' I asked pointing west towards the same place. 'No one knows,'…was the reply. 'At least know one knows for sure. No one ever goes there….It's a cursed place….But no! No need all that….Now, ma'am why don't you have your wash now. It's getting late and Mr. Lloyd is very prompt'…. 'Please, Ophelia but what?'…. 'I am not sure if I should say this to you Ma'am'….She stopped and hesitated for a while. But I tried to show that I was quite eager…..'Well, Ophelia what harm could it ever cause, I am just an outcast…. But if it's a secret….I totally understand. I was just curious, that's all'…..'Oh, my! Ma'am….Well you see it's a bad place, not safe either. There are rumors saying that the place is haunted. But nothing is specified. Some even say that…. Oh my…' then she lowered her voice and said… 'Some even say that the late Mr. and Mrs. Anderson along with their two baby girls met into an accident in that very same spot,' then she broke into chills…. 'Some even say that it

wasn't an accident but an attempted murder....'
she broke down into chills. I was listening to all
this with great interest, my ears pierced. 'But
Ophelia....What happened next?' Then
suddenly she came closer to me and
whispered into my ear as if even the walls were
listening.... 'Mr. and Mrs. Anderson died'....
Again she paused and made a strange
sound.... 'Some say Mr. and Mrs. Anderson
were a wicked lot but people respected them
as they were top nobility, I guess their wealth
was an attraction. But surely, they weren't quite
good. Miss. Rachel's behavior says it all.' She
examined me closely. 'Well Ophelia, the two
babies did they die too?' I exclaimed. 'Oh,
ma'am It's so sad,' she said wiping some
imaginary tears from under her eye and giving
out a sniffing sound in order to make the
situation seem live—'One died, one survived
and that's Miss.Rachel, she owns the property
now that she is almost twenty one. Until then,

all of it will be officially handled by our dear Mr. Lloyd, he had always been in the family ever since the late Andersons, and he surely is a dear and very honest too….' she paused again. She had gotten used to speaking with me now and her tone was no longer official. 'Then Ophelia….What happened to the other girl child? Is she really dead?'…. 'Oh ma'am and she broke into chills again, all are rumors….but some do say she was only half dead and still lingers around that old place. Miss. Rachel did try her level best to find her in the last few years yet nothing had come out of it,' she murmured. 'So she was never found,' I added. 'Nope, never!' she shrieked. 'But we all wish that this lost sister could be revealed,' 'Why Ophelia?' I asked. My curiosity was much more than I could handle now. Yet, Ophelia became silent…'What Ophelia?' I asked. 'That child… Miss. Rachel is quiet icy, she acts to her own will; she is uncontrollable, insolent and extremely rude. It's quite a challenge to be with her....But the poor thing, who could blame her... She has had no family ever since she was born, no love, no care and no affection. There was nothing but trouble in her life. First her parents and then her sister....' she paused again and looked at me. 'You seemed to be interested ma'am.' That was quite sudden and I didn't really expect it. 'Oh....Oh yeah!' but again said that I was interested and insists that she carry on. And surprisingly she did...'You seen ma'am, that old place is quite important to the Andersons and Miss. Rachel visits there once every fortnight, she never takes anyone along with her....Mr. Lloyd had always tried to tag along but he is constantly refused....' she came closer to me again, close to my ear and whispered,.... 'There is a legend; people who have got separated from that lonely spot will surely meet again! It's probably even when the world ends but for them it's where a new world begins....' then again she stopped....'I am not sure if I'm supposed to be telling you this but you'll probably know soon enough, Miss. Rachel had recently got into a near fatal accident. Some say it was attempted too but no one could prove it,' she stopped again but resumed...'Mr. Lloyd wasn't here either or he could never have let that happen....unfortunately, he had gone to London the previous night.' I was listening to all of these with great astonishment; Ophelia too was buoyant by this sudden new interest. She continued...making the foreseen tale much more engrossing. 'The poor little thing, she used to be a child prodigy....her talent for the arts cannot be expressed in words, it was pure talent....she had just turned professional when this happened. I guess fate had wronged her again. Then this incident got her confined into the room. She is differently abled now, a complete wreck....doctors had given up hope in her. They said she would never make a full recovery. Miss. Rachel had to give up her carrier. That poor child….She really was passionate about that dance of hers'….she paused. 'Now ma'am here comes the most exciting part....on the day of the accident; Miss. Rachel claims that she had been saved by a spirit from above. 'WHAT!' I exclaimed. My heart skipped a beat and started pounding heavily. 'WHAT, a spirit!' I questioned back trying to keep my voice as normal as I could. 'But they don't exist, do they?'

'Yeah ma'am....we doubt that too, due to this…. rumors have spread that the Great Miss. Rachel Ingramme Anderson Turner had gone bonkers....but then again, she whispered... 'It's not totally false though, Miss. Rachel did suffer from brain damage yet we believe she is not mad, just shaken that's all. Hmm….all are just rumors, they normally do spread faster than wildfire. 'She paused and the rest was accompanied by an awkward silence. I guessed that was the end of the tale. Mrs. Ophelia was glancing at me without blinking. Then she returned to her strange tone again and said 'You see ma'am, recently Miss. Rachel jabbers continuously about her sister telling about dreams or something like ...' Just then a bell rang.....echoing throughout the manor, filling the room while shooing away the silence and solitary of the room. 'It's the bell for breakfast,' shrieked Ophelia. 'I am sorry ma'am, I talk too much. Mr. Lloyd would be expecting you anytime soon,' I could feel the struggle in her voice as she spoke. Curious though I was, I decided not to question anything more....This conversation was really interesting....yet, it did go a bit too far and we kind of lost track of time. Without a word, I advanced towards the wash basin standing in the far corner of the room. By now, the soothing hot water in it had gone cold......I checked my reflection in the mirror attached to the wall. The haunted eyes and the dark circles underneath them made the long, drawn in face almost unrecognizable. I waved my hand and the person waved back. Good! I sighed. I am still me, nothing had changed. Finally, my heart started pounding in the normal pace and as the cold water brushed my face I felt great. It had been quite a long time since I felt such comfort. The past few days of my life had been nothing but trouble. Ophelia stood next to me while I got dressed in an old fashioned long brown frock with a small white collar. I dressed as how I was told and since this was my first time trying human clothing, I found it to be very similar to what I wore as an angel. The black silk robe which I had worn earlier lay devastated on the floor, completely ruined. I picked it up, folded it and laid it gently on the long wooden table since it was the only thing that reminded me I was an angel. Later, I took a comb and brushed my hair very smooth. Finally, I was ready. 'How do I look?' I questioned Ophelia. 'Fair as a lily,' she answered. You look quite different ma'am; you were quite a wreck when we first found you.' Reader, with all this excitement and anxiety I forget to tell you about Ophelia. Well, to be precise there was nothing special about her just the ordinary happy-go lucky type woman about thirty years in age. The servant seemed a placid, good natured and phlegmatic woman. But she was a solid square figure with no shape at all with dark eyes, short curled hair and red cheeks like apples. Her face was plain and hard as an Indian rubber ball, she was a nice woman in many ways and I was instantly drawn to her. I preferred her over to Mr. Lloyd who also seemed nice but in his own ways. 'Ophelia….What happens next?' I exclaimed. The sound of the turning doorknob could be heard and suddenly the door creaked and opened widely. I expected it to be Mr. Lloyd but yet standing there was a timid mouse–like girl of about sixteen or seventeen. 'What now Shelby?' asked Ophelia. But the girl turned away from her and stared at me instead. 'Sir Lloyd would be glad to see Miss Stranger in the drawing room please, 'she stuttered in her small voice still gawking at my face timidly. 'Thanks, Shelby you may go,' said Ophelia but the girl didn't obey her. She just stood close to the door, staring at my face as if I was the most unusual thing in the world and it felt awkward. Yet, I smiled at her but she didn't return it but left with the same impression in which she had first came in. 'Whoa, Shelby Millers' said Ophelia. She helps Mrs. Carton with the cooking; the girl lives nearby in a cottage close to the woods but don't take much notice of her. Nice little thing but not the chatty type, much more of a mouse. Yet Mr. Lloyd took her in. He is very generous and kind to the poor and Feed

The Hungry is his law,' said Ophelia as we left the room together and walked across the incredibly grand corridor with its dark walnut floors and old carved chests which stood on either sides of the dimly lit corridor, giving it an air of antiquity. As we were climbing up the staircase with stairs and banister made of oak, I suddenly asked from Ophelia who was by now almost my friend 'what is Mr. Lloyd like?' There was a short pause. 'He is the greatest, most tender-hearted person you will ever meet,' was the reply. 'Even though, he can be quite peculiar at times because he disappears quite too often now and then. Yet, there's no one like him. He is the best. But beware of Miss Rachel, the mistress of this grand manor because she's not very forgiving.' By this talk, later on only I got to know that it was Mr. Lloyd who had taken me in the first place itself. 'Ma'am, I almost forgot,' said Ophelia. 'What? 'I asked. 'What's your name? Who are you and where are you from?' But she was cut short as we had already reached the door, I had expected a thick paneled huge door yet it was an old creaky one with a huge sense of melancholy and I wondered why? Yet, Ophelia repeated herself 'Ma'am I forget to ask, who you are or what are you?' I turned to her and opened my mouth to speak yet no words came out. Several questions flooded my brain, this is what Mr. Lloyd too would probably ask first, oh no! I thought. I had completely forgotten to create a cock and bull story. What to do now? Several thoughts suddenly flowed into my head. Surely, I couldn't give away the fact that I am a stranded angel on a mission. 'Well ma'am,' inquired Ophelia. I looked at her and smiled yet she was waiting eagerly for a reply and I knew that being silent would probably give the game away. 'I am an orphan,' were the first words which came to me and I struggled to create a story but much to my own relief we were standing in front of the drawing room door. 'Mr. Lloyd is waiting,' I said in a faintish tone. 'Oh! Yeah, sorry......I almost forgot,' said Ophelia. She went forward and gave a light tap on the door which was almost inaudible. I didn't expect a reply but out came a rough voice, Mr. Lloyd's voice. 'Enter!' he said gruffly and I reluctantly went in.....Wow! I was completely marveled by the exquisite beauty of the room. I did expect a luxurious type room but this! This was totally out of the world and definitely out of my wildest expectations. It was elegant, no!

It was more than that. Magnificent! I thought. The walls were hung with fine grey canvas, there was a large silvery grey carpet and the furniture was covered with dark green silky material. Omega cushions and the pictures exploded their colours....In this room too there were ornaments of bohemian glass, ruby red and gleaming. The room was warm and comfortable looking but what attracted me the most was the huge table laid out with wide varieties of scrumptious food and eatables and standing just beside it was a familiar figure in the dark corner, away from the lighted area but I couldn't see his face. My heart started pounding unevenly....this figure was somewhat familiar; I had seen him somewhere before I became a human. But where could it ever be? 'Here is the girl, sir' said Ophelia in a slightly official voice, sounding serious. The figure came forward to the lighted area of the room and I noticed the stern face. It was Mr. Lloyd. 'Leave us alone, please!' he said glaring at Ophelia and making a movement from his hand towards the door in dismissal. My heart jumped into my mouth again and I could feel the tingling sensation in my feet. Ophelia instantly obeyed the order as she seemed to have a great respect towards this man; she gave a low bow and departed. I could hear the door closing and she was gone. We were left alone? I could feel the tension in the air. Yet, my eyes drifted towards the enormous table. I guess Mr. Lloyd must have noticed since he smiled and invited me to be seated and I thankfully did. The thought of sinking my teeth into a decent meal after a very long time, felt just great. I was ravenous. I wasn't normally the polite type but yet I waited impatiently until Mr. Lloyd asked me to eat. Mr Lloyd had been examining my face. 'Dig in!' he said. And no more was said. There was no need to tell me twice and as those words leaked out of his mouth, I started to gobble up the treats without any hesitation. Gulping down whatever was on my way. How I ate? I ate a great deal. Mr. Lloyd didn't utter a word and I was glad. Yet, he was examining me. Finally, I became better and returned to my normal happy self. The food was like nectar and ambrosia. Still, Mr. Lloyd didn't say a word….he jut stood still like a doomed statue. Finally, eating was done and the coffee was bought in by a maid who I hadn't seen before. As I sat on the winged chair, sipping my portion of coffee instead of gulping it down, Mr. Lloyd drew himself up to his full height....yet, he didn't speak. He just stood looking into the cheerful blazing fire, and in the light of the fire shone his strong features and the large dark eyes which looked very fine, honest and kind very unlike his face. His eyes drifted away from the fire towards me and finally, the moment I had been dreading arrived. He spoke....in a father-like tone and I was astounded by the calmness and soothing nature in it. I didn't expect much kindness from him.....'How are you now?' 'Much better sir thanks....' I knew that I had to be careful with my answers. I shouldn't give away any true facts I thought....Best to careful, I wished I could get away now; a slip in tongue and my whole life will be in stake. My whole life depended on this…. I had to be extra careful. He came closer towards me………my heart pounded, I could hear a slight buzzing noise inside my head and I kind of felt like throwing up. He was silent for a moment or two….then he spoke…. 'What's your name child and what's your purpose? 'Things were starting to happen now. 'Ivy'….I answered. 'Ivy Splencer….' but I couldn't understand what he meant by asking my purpose…. 'What happened?' he inquired. 'Why were you lying on the middle of the dark and eerie woods, alone and fainted?...aren't you aware….Child….you could have died…. it was a miracle that I happened to pass by, It isn't accustomed for a young girl of your age to be out that late at night either.' He paused. 'Well, sir thanks for everything….I owe you my life. Thanks a lot!'…. 'Don't deflect the question, child….what were you doing out in the woods and don't lie!'

The words popped out of my mouth, quicker than I had expected. 'I am an orphan sir.....I have no family.' 'Any uncles, aunts or relatives,' he questioned. 'I have none and never had either'.... I answered. His voice softened.... 'Oh! Sorry about that, I thought you were a runaway.'

'No need to be sorry sir, I am thankful. I really am.' 'Please...continue!' he said. He took his eyes away from my face and returned to gaze back at the fire. 'Let's hear your full story,' he said taking his own cup of coffee into his hand and sipping it slowing. I cudgeled my smarts, I felt my body burning from inside. Of course, I couldn't tell him my true story. Various thoughts flooded my head....but there was something else bothering my mind now....but I wasn't completely sure what it is. I had heard Mr. Lloyd's voice somewhere before and it felt familiar like I had heard it somewhere before I was turned into a human. But that couldn't be, where could I have heard or seen Mr. Lloyd before….Impossible….I thought. Never! There's no way! 'I am waiting,' echoed the impatient voice. 'Excuse me sir, what did you say' He made an impatient movement but…'I am waiting to hear your full story, my child. Make it clear and don't add anything.' I was in for a tough time now. Mr. Lloyd was serious and there's no escape now. 'I am an orphan sir….I have no family or friends…. I am all alone in this dark world sir…. I grew up in a church….' 'So you're a nun?' he questioned. 'No sir,' I explained. 'I just stayed there, the high priest took me in when I was just a child and I had been living there ever since. Recently, I did something bad. Well sir, it wasn't that bad but anyway they kicked me out….I was alone, hungry and without a care in the world. I wanted to find my own living yet, it wasn't that easy. I didn't have a home or a place to go so I walked and walked….for days....for nights. Many days passed. I was tired, hungry and faintish and finally I fell.' Those words just spilled out of my mouth quicker than excepted. Some way or another, I wished that he would let me stay here. Then I could see to Miss Rachel, finish my mission and return home. Up to now, Mr. Lloyd had been listening to my story without questioning a single thing. He just listened.... 'Well....sir...that's it....that's my story. I guess, after that you found me laying on the ground and took me in.' I expected him to speak but he didn't. He just stared at my face, time went by but neither of us spoke. I felt impatient yet I didn't dare to open my mouth. More time passed....I became more and more impatient. Yet I knew I had to wait for his reply, impatient though I was. More time passed, and then finally he spoke....As the words spilled out of his mouth....I waited in eagerness for his reply. 'How old are you?' 'I am twenty Sir,' I answered hastily. 'And you are looking for work?' 'Yes sir,' I said still holding my breath. 'Have you had any experience? I mean how your schooling days were?' he asked. 'No sir, I haven't had any. Yet, I am willing to do anything. I could do the cooking, cleaning, sewing or anything if you would let me stay, sir.' I said without even stopping to breath. 'Please, let me stay sir'…. 'I am willing to, my child'….he said and then he paused. 'I am just a manager of this house,' and then again there was a pause. There was a sudden bitterness in his voice as talked about the ownership….there was silence again. He spoke again. 'You see, my child. The owner of this house Miss. Rachel Ingramme Anderson Turner is not present today and will be returning after a month. But then… he paused again while he examined my eagerly waiting face. 'Okay! You are in!' he exclaimed suddenly. You will help Ophelia in the kitchen, is it okay with you?' he asked. 'I'll be more than happy sir, how could I ever repay you?' 'Okay then, that's settled….you may stay as long as you like….I will tell Miss. Rachel as soon as she returns'….'Thank you sir! Thanks a lot! I will never for once forget what you have done'…. 'You may go, leave then.' he said his voice suddenly hardening up again. 'DISMISSED!' he roared.

As days flew by ….

For some time, my days passed on without much interest. Sooner or later, I knew that I had to get adapted to my new life. Anderson manor was a lonely old place, very solemn and I was alone for most of the time. Nothing happened out of the usual. Yet on the whole, I was contented to be there. Of course, the work was hard at first but everyone was quite friendly and I learned fast. I got chances to experience various new things from cooking to washing, things that I had never heard or seen before. Still, there was no sign of Miss. Rachel Ingramme Anderson Turner. Where had she gone? I was dying to meet her and as days went on, I became eager and eager....Yet, nothing happened as my days kept going on. I had begun to love Anderson manor, it felt like a home and I soon got attached to it. I began to cherish every little detail in it. Feelings that I've never experienced before crowded my body, the feeling of love and attachment to a certain place. Time flew. My life as an angel was getting further and further away from me. I had finally got the type of home, I had always dreamed of. I had no intention in returning to my heavenly realm. It felt like the past and this no longer felt like a punishment. I was happy. Yet, my mission hadn't even begun yet....It felt like I was fated to be here, Anderson manor became my home.

The air of a home from the past....a shrine of memory....

6. The Mistress of the House

The sound of bare emptiness in my solitary room was disrupted by the loud gregarious boom of thunder rolling through the sky as another lightning bolt split the sky into two. It sounded like the heavens were about to fall and God-in-charge playing a game of football with Professor Pete. I stood near my window pane waiting to wash the misery away. I stood there all alone but happy. I stood there my gaze burning into the horizon, staring at the peculiar beauty of the upcoming storm. The day had simply been dark, gloomy and overcast but in seconds it became a wall of water. Here come the liquid globes that reflected the greenery of nature, falling from the sky of grey velvet. It was exactly the sort of weather that washes everything anew painting together a new picture that was totally different from the previous days. It fell like endless buckets of water as if the heavenly realms were crying their hearts out. 'Let it come!'….my heart cried out. I was in my new home. 'Let it come! Fall down to the earth as much as you can!' I cried. To feel it scattering along my body wasn't enjoyment but yet staring with my eyes wide open on a cold, caliginous day inside a warm room surely felt great. And in that moment of happy congregation came the sense of being alive. 'Human life surely was good!' As time flew…The icy grey sky rumbled restlessly little by little turning into a disorientated chaos. The sprinkling in no time at all turned into a torrential downpour pouring down into the earth with a roar, knocking on the doors and window panes like a flamboyant guest. Little by little, the water droplets got larger and larger….becoming in the size of olive pits as it hammers down on my window like the relentless drumming of nails….obscuring my view of the world beyond while the pitter patter sound crackled like an old radio coming to life…….I stood near my window still glaring hungrily at the magnificent sight, but soon the bone-chilling cold became unbearable. I could already feel the dampness within my bones and the coldness that crept over my skin, yet I wasn't even wet. I stood there for another second or two but as the clouds continued crying restlessly. I decided to retire into the warm cosines of my bed. I wanted to turn in for the day….And walked away from the window, still wondering where this Rachel Ingramme Anderson Turner could have gone. I burrowed myself into the thick, soft sheets like a bear in hibernation still listening to the melancholic song outside created while the wind whipped the frigid drops, sending them hurtling in every possible direction. The rain was enchanting, yet I wasn't fortunate enough to stay any longer and I dissolved into a deep slumber....

'I was not alone but in an unknown road. I was lost. I was close to death and looked extremely pale. But, there was another girl alongside with me. But that wasn't me. I was only a baby. Twenty years younger, it was a younger version of me however the baby was me and I was sure of it. There was another child, a girl about my own age with chestnut colored hair and a pale face. We were holding our hands tightly together but we were both weak. We weren't strong enough to stay together....The other infant was drifting further and further away....into an unknown path. I was crying, begging for us to remain together but she, the other child was disappearing and I was left alone in the howling wind and god in charge of death asking me to come to his embrace. I was alone! The pain was becoming unbearable and a scream was torn out from my chest. Then everything shattered. I began to cry, louder and louder….god-in charge was there now….standing in front of me like a doomed statue…. and he asked me to choose….an angel or a human?'

'HELP ME! Help me!' I screamed from the top of my lungs and 'thud!' I woke up….to find out I was no longer in my cozy bed but in the cold floor entangled within the sheet covers, I had fallen! My heart flooded with relief, it was only a dream, a nightmare! The room was dark, it was midnight as I heard the old grandfather clock struck twelve….the room was dark and I needed a light so desperately. So, I outstretched my hand down the locker to find one….yet it was a fruitless attempt as the locker was empty. I stretched my hand down the bed and was only too delighted to find a Bunsen burner. How had it got down there? I thought, yet I reached over to turn the base, to feed it with oxygen and at once the fire became golden and took the shape of a flower head. I watched the many petals becoming more distant, folding outward while radiating the light and warmth. It lit the room with its blazing flame; I got back up on my bed and tried to sleep. I knew many techniques for falling asleep, I tried them all. By now I was convinced that doing them would only keep me awake longer....and finally I gave up any attempt to sleep. 'I guess it was another long sleepless night.' I muttered to myself. I stood up straight....the powerful feeling of the dream stayed with me, lingering unshakably in the air. Thinking back, it was the same dream that I had seen the first day I arrived at Anderson manor. It felt so real that various questions flew around my head like a cartoon of flying birds....Was it just a strange dream or was it a reality? For a few moments, I lived in a strange world. Was it just a dream or hallucination or was I seeing the past and future but these feelings didn't last long as something very anomalous was about to happen.......I heard a strange sound. It seemed as if someone was walking right outside my room. I heard the sound of light footsteps but the sound was getting further and further away. What could it be? No one ever comes to this part of the house, do they? Especially not in the midnight anyway, was it a burglar? I stayed glued to my bed, daring not to move. I could hear the sound again....Much heavier now. 'Who's there?' I called. There was no answer. I was cold with fear and my blood turned into flowing water....I wished that the footsteps would go away.... 'Maybe, its Ophelia'....I thought and it calmed me 'Maybe Shelby or Mrs. Carton.' My nerves relaxed....but again, footsteps could be heard....by now, I was sure it was neither of them as the footsteps were so heavy that the sound echoed through the hallway....I was nervous and tried to hold my breath and think straight …….. 'Who's there?' I cried. 'Shelby? Ophelia? Mrs. Carton, is that you?' Yet no one answered. I gulped….Who could it be? Why isn't anyone answering? If it had been in the middle of the day or evening I would have been much less frightened…. yet it was midnight, the time when the ghosts lingered around….The footsteps could be heard again now in the stairs. With much hesitation….I finally gathered up my thoughts…. 'Who's there?' I cried for the very last time. My thoughts were now gathered into one place. 'You can do it, Ivy! Come on! Still shaking with horror and alarm, I put on my dressing gown….and slowly tip-toed onto the gallery….trying to make as little sound as possible. I slowly opened my door and as the door creaked, out came a sound like something falling and my insides seemed to stand still. Yet, I wasn't backing off…. 'It's now or never!' I exclaimed and opened the door as quickly as I could with my eyes tightly closed and jumped into the gallery 'On guard!' I was ready to fight. I opened my eyes….yet no one was there….the gallery was empty, dark and still. There was nothing out of the usual. The entire household was completely still. 'Who's there?' I cried again, now in an almost whisper….No one answered for a moment or two. I wondered if I was just imagining things and the footsteps were only part of my dream. Yet no, I heard the sound again….someone surely was walking down the steps….this wasn't any kind of dream for sure. It was reality. But, who could it be? Who would come here in the dead of night? Was it a thief? I advanced….but slowly, trying not to make a single sound….I continued advancing slowly and steadily as if I was afraid of waking up the dead….as I kept going further….I could see something down on the floor….broken and shattered. It was a bohemian glass,….Someone surely was here….he or she must have heard the creak on my door as it opened, felt nervous and   dropped this by mistake. But who could it be? Someone had been here and I knew it, I felt it in my bones….I could feel sweat bending down on my forehead as I walked around the corner and my heart threatened to burst out from its rib case. I could hear the footsteps again; moving somewhere close by….I went down the steps and the banisters of oak while my head buzzed as if a swarm of bees were around it. I continued advancing….the footsteps could still be heard, drifting further and further away. I was so anxious. 'Who could it be? Whose there?' I cried. I moved on….I was very close to the door that leads outside the manor. 'Whose there?' I cried. The footsteps stopped and I heard the backdoor open and close very slowly…. I was very close to the door now. I paused….Should I go out. Could it be dangerous? Well…On the second thought, of course. The curiosity flooded through my body, until it became almost unbearable. The sound of footsteps could no longer be heard but instead what I heard later on….Was the very last thing I could ever have expected….Someone was outside for sure, I thought and went closer to the door and stood there for a moment or two. Something could be heard….It was a familiar voice and I recognized it at once….He was swearing to god in a trembling voice. 'Circumstances had made me evil! God take me away. I can't handle this any longer,' boomed the voice. I was baffled. What was going on? I silently held the doorknob and twisted it gently. I opened the door just enough so I could see what was going on…. 'I am a sinner!' the voice screamed. There was indescribable sadness in it and tons of grief….the person was cursing himself. Hot torrents of grief cursed down on his face. He was screaming, He mumbled several incoherent things which I couldn't hear properly….A carousel of thoughts flooded my head….I decided to step out. By now, much to own relief the downpour had stopped…. And the sky had cleared. As I walked across the slippery stone path, I listened. 'Revenge is the disaster, hatred is the matter. Fate had wronged me. Please, god! You have always been unfair. Help me die without any pain!' he cried. He cursed himself. 'What's going on?' I thought as I walked forward. I couldn't make out head or tail about these strange happenings. What was he saying? The man cursed and cursed. He screamed and how he screamed....He seemed so different from how I had first seen him. What had happened to the rough, stern but yet ever so tender-hearted gentleman? What had happened and what was happening to my savior now? Once his first tear had broken, free tears stripped down and overflowed like a river escaping a dam. His face was filled with raw emotions while his chin trembled. His lips trembled while he cried….More and more gut wrenching tears tore through his face. A great tremor overtook him. He was praying and uttering phrases that I couldn't hear. More and more tears poured out from deep inside his chest. Yet he prayed. He screamed….He seemed like a psycho. He clenched his fists tightly together and screamed. 'Why? Why is life so unfair?' He could handle the heartbreak no longer and he fell to the floor as a disheveled heap while his grief flooded in uncontrollable tears. I was devastated! It was painful to see him like this. I was heartbroken.... My body felt entangled yet I straightened my face and continued to move towards his direction....This wasn't something I had expected from him. By now, I had developed great respect and honor towards him but what's this? What was happening?

Still, he hadn't noticed my appearance....I decided to console him in anyway I could....I gathered up the courage to speak to him....

'Excuse me, sir....Mr. Lloyd Sir....What's wrong sir....Is there anything I can do to help? What's wrong sir?'

He stood up as if he was struck by a lightning shock. He looked dumbfounded! He covered his face and tried to hold the torrent of tears that gushed out without control....He wiped his eyes which were red and swollen by now....There was such grief in his face. He looked shocked! He surely hadn't expected my appearance....'EVIL IS THE MATTER – WRONGDOING IS THE MATTER! THE WORLD IS CRUEL!' I've never seen a man so excited. He seemed so changed! Where was the gentleman–type man, I've first met! He was electrified! He ran into the house. What just happened? Oh, my.... I was left to my own thoughts....

In the morning: After a sleepless night accompanied by a slight catnap....I was up, before five o' clock the next morning of the 28th of July. I tided myself up and looked out of the windowsill and as I did, I thought of my life. The present was vague and strong, and of the future I could guess nothing....It was like I had no future....For sometime, my life had been quite sheltered and action-free, but now not anymore....I felt as if anything could happen now....There was a strange air of despondency within myself but I couldn't identify from what or where it came from....I stepped out of my room,....into the silent gallery, nothing had changed. Everything was so grand, stately and with it's air of antiquity.... just the same old stuff but yet no matter how I think about it, the happenings last night would not leave my head.....I descended down the stairs and stepped out of the half-open door ,onto the great gardens of Anderson Manor. It was a bright and beautiful day, the sun resolutely below the horizon....I looked up at the crimson sky and for the first time I thought about my heavenly realm, of my duties as an Angel....Of Professor Pete.... My mission ... which hadn't even started yet..... I felt bitter.... Hours flew by ... And at last heard a bell ringing... echoing through the Manor to wake everyone up, to start another day.... My head was filled with several thoughts and 'what ifs' I turned to go.... I stopped... I looked up.... There stood Anderson Manor, The old – century mansion looming proudly behind the thick iron gates, flanked by rows of skeletal trees crowned in crimson accompanied by perfectly manicured hedges. The house was red – brick Victorian and beautifully symmetrical, two wings stretching to either sides. There was an open porch at the front, held up with the most ostentatiously detailed pillars painted in brilliant white and in its threshold stood a delicate

marble fountain. It surely was one fine place....
'Ivy!' called a hard plain voice. It was Mr. Lloyd.
I wasn't ready to face him just yet but I gave
him a weak smile. 'Ivy!' he called out. 'Coming
sir,' I added as I went towards him. Before I
could speak....He said.... 'Pardon me for the
excitement last night, please accept my
apology if I startled you,' he exclaimed. But yet
he wasn't his usual self....What could have
happened to change him so much. 'I was just
surprised, sir. Are you okay? How do you feel
sir?' he paused.....'Very well, thanks'....He
seemed so strange. I definitely saw a change,
something which made it difficult for me to be
friendly with him. 'Well....Then, if you'd excuse
me,' he turned to leave. 'Wait sir. What
happened last night?' The words dropped out
of my mouth like a pistol–shot. He glared at
me....then answered reluctantly....'I was sleep
– walking.' Without waiting for more he walked
off..... 'What's with him, I thought. 'Sleep

walking.... huh....really. Does he think I am a fool or something?'....

I returned back to the house and into the dining room to have breakfast. 'Where did you go off.... so early in the morning?' asked Ophelia as I entered. 'To get some fresh air,'... I said joining her. 'Ophelia, 'I asked. 'Have you noticed anything strange....I mean in Mr. Lloyd?' 'Mr. Lloyd!' she exclaimed, 'Why? He just left for London,.' she said again. 'Where did he go?' I questioned back. 'London,' was the answer. 'He said he had some matters to take care of.' We were already finished with breakfast when Shelby came....with a letter in her right hand. She handed it over to Ophelia who tore it open.... I watched eagerly..... 'It's from Madam Rachel Ingramme Anderson Turner. She'll be coming home within the next fortnight. We are in for a rough time,' added Ophelia. 'God be praised!' I thought. At last....

7. How Time Went By?

Reader….Up to now I've been going on in detail about my early life but since this story cannot get any longer. I'll pass on about what happened with only a couple of lines to note the changes that came to pass.....The fortnight passed on rapidly and ultimately Rachel Ingramme Anderson Turner arrived. I had been dying to meet her and now she was finally here. But after she arrived it didn't feel that great. She was a bossy girl, very difficult to be with. For many times a day ...I wondered if my mission could ever be completed. Miss. Rachel wasn't that pleased with me either. For most of the time she ignored me and asked me to leave her house and get lost. But as time flew by, we got closer and closer....I began to love her and on the day she poured out her story to me…. I felt happy that she had confided in me. I grew attached to her….But one gloomy night something very peculiar happened………..

A fire broke....destroying almost everything. I was unable to help Rachel but then something else happened....As I struggled to help her.....I saw a light. Yet, I struggled. Then suddenly my good deeds came back to me.......I couldn't believe my eyes....The wild-boy, the fourteen year old gawky red haired teen appeared out of nowhere....'I have come to help you miss,' he said. It's a gift from a "Friend from Far" and believe it or not he did help us. We were both saved, me and Rachel. Yet, Anderson Manor was destroyed completely. A few days later,

We found out that the fire was attempted....an attempted murder to be exact. Mr. Lloyd had caused it. He was just a man in disguise, a man in a veil. As time went by,

We also learned that he was the 'stranger in black', the very person who had tried to kill Rachel in the car accident in the first place itself. It surely was a devastating shock! After this incident, we got much more attached. Various circumstances made us realize that we were true sisters after all...

But since, she opened up to me, my mission was completed and I had to leave. It wasn't my will and I didn't want to leave her either.

So what happened next?

8. 6 Years Later, Endings

I Gave up my life. My fantasy life as an Angel. I am no longer an Angel. Yet, however I am not disappointed at the very least. And I never would be either. I got something much better than my own life, a sister... a person to love, a person to cherish and a person I want to spend the rest of my life with........

To be with her was my life. To be with her was my happiness and only joy. This was the one and only thing I could do for her, for her to be happy, for her to live. And if she is happy, I am sure I will be too. This was the easiest thing I could do for my beloved sister. It was to throw myself away. Live for her. Be with her. That is life, happy life.

Up to now I have been recalling my life story, about how I fell from the sky and finally ended up on living in the place of my destiny…Don't you like an ending like this? We overcame all of life's difficulties, hardships with love, determination and courage and then all the mysteries got solved. But my story won't end just yet….No! Not quite like this! Reader, Hold on a bit longer cause everything will end very soon… hold just a bit more….

It was a bright sunny day as I wandered across the woods. How I looked forward to seeing my beloved sister! Like a lover who was eager to see her lover's face without waking her up I wanted to see her smile, to hug her tightly and to tell her the good news I am "OFFICIALLY HUMAN!" And that I could stay beside her forever. As I walked across the woods, my heart skipped a beat, not that I am nervous or anything but of extreme happiness. I continued advancing….And finally reached the gigantic Iron Gate and Anderson Manner! How happy I was to be back home again, home sweet home I was finally there! Yet instead of the grand, aristocratic manor house laid a sympathetic ruin. A blackened ruin completely destroyed by that night's incident. I stood there....for a moment or two, it was a devastating sight! Yet, I didn't feel sad. At least, no one died and that's what matters the most. The columns were the only complete thing, everything else had crumbled but yet a light shone in from one of the corner rooms which had not been burned down completely. From that, I could get a glimpse of a lonely, isolated figure. It none other than my angelic sister! I wanted to run up to her, yet I stopped...and as I gazed at the manor a bit longer.... I got a reminder of the fire, of Mr. Lloyd and his story. The man who helped me in the first place, the kindhearted man who took me in....My savior....It was much better to think that the fire was an accident rather than accepting the bitter truth. Yet, no one could alter the past....only the future matters. What is done is done and nobody could change that! The ones who are destined to remain with us will always remain, no one tear them apart not even god while others will pass by silently. The silence of death was there and the solicitude of tragedy. The place of my origin was a blackened skeleton, a thick scar which had no intension of healing. Without thinking any more I continued advancing......

There wasn't a front door any more, all had been burnt down and while climbing up the crumbling staircase my heart sobbed. I was so excited. I finally reached her door and slowly opened it.....It was a small, shabby room broken down and ruined. Only one wall stood, black and ugly, the others were jagged and low too stubborn to fall just yet, the room was brightly lit with candle flames and as I entered.

my sight! I don't need you; I'll live a life of a nun. Go Away!' She roared….This wasn't really what I expected, yet I stared blankly. I knew she didn't actually meant what she just said…Then unexpectedly, she ran in to my arms….and began to cry while her tears wetted my clothes. I did not know what to do, yet I stroked her hair gently….Finally, she calmed down and we sat by the fireside, together now.

'What happened to Mr. Lloyd,' was my immediate question. She paused…. Then looked away….. I knew then that my worst fear was now turned into reality. 'He killed himself,' was the faint reply. That was a shock! I used to respect him a lot but he deserved it anyway….Nothing could be done now. It was the past! 'Enough about him now,' my sister said. 'Let's talk about us. What happened? Are you really human? But how could it be?' I poured out my story and she listened as if it was the most interesting thing in the world. 'And you?' I questioned back....

'I was dying; I will not smile. I will not live a good life. I will be the least happy person in the world. I will not have anyone. I will scoff at anyone speaking about family. I will forever live alone. I said these things to myself,' my sister said. And we embraced each other again....much more affectionately this time.

'It will never happen again,' I repeated.

'Let's be together forever,' she said. 'But not here, there are too many bad memories in this place....Let us go somewhere peaceful and quieter.'

06 Years Later...

'Among the many words that I have learned after coming here, the best words are as of now in this moment is a "Happy Ending". But the hopes and despair that life gives you is that time keeps flowing and moments pass. Behind that moment of brilliant happiness, no one knows what kind of moments await'....

'Ivy!' called my sister.

'What!' I asked....

'Will our story have a happy ending?' she asked. 'Ivy! Let's end this story here since we are both happy, I really do not want our story to have a mourning end....'

(Reader, Another chapter is closing but our life won't end here. And as we are together it will always be a happy ending.)

Even when one door closes ,another door opens....When one person leaves, we encounter someone even better....When thousands of good moments fly by ,at least one will be heartbreaking but never doubt the rest....We will whole-heartedly live our life to the fullest and will always remember to move ahead....

'Finally, we made our dream come true in a village where not much exists, not much news occurs in a small boring village. With nothing special having a very simple life while laughing and crying at the simplest things….Being happy, being sad while quietly watching our time fly by. I have had enough drama to last a lifetime, each day, each hour, each minute, each second wondering about the happiness of life, after taking many detours, in this hard fought road. It was treasury, the love that finally came to me. It is destiny! It is fate! It is a secret as we remember our legend that is far off, beautiful, charming and secretive. It is a CRASH LANDING. It is,

Life of an Angel - The end.

AUTHOR BIO

167

"Life of an Angel" is the debut novel of the teenage author Vidara Liyanage. The 14 year old author was born in a small town in Colombo, Sri Lanka. She is currently studying in I-Gate College, Colombo and is a ninth grader. The young author is hoping to write more in the near future and sincerely hopes that her very first novel would become a good leap for her future works to come.

www.ingramcontent.com/pod-product-compliance
Lightning Source LLC
LaVergne TN
LVHW051526170726
843492LV00006B/1651